More Praise for

THE

CENTER

OF

EVERYTHING

"Ruby's large imagination and even bigger heart are beautifully evoked." —*Publishers Weekly*

★ "A poignant, finely wrought exploration of grief."
—*Kirkus Reviews,* starred review

"Give this to patient readers who enjoy Polly Horvath's *The Vacation* (2005) and *Everything on a Waffle* (2001)."
—*School Library Journal*

★ "This is a terrific first step up for kids who are just beginning to explore more complicated novels."
—*The Bulletin,* starred review

THE
CENTER
OF
EVERYTHING

Linda Urban

◉

HOUGHTON MIFFLIN HARCOURT
Boston   New York

For information about permission to reproduce selections from this book,
write to Permissions, Houghton Mifflin Harcourt Publishing Company,
215 Park Avenue South, New York, New York 10003.

www.hmhco.com

The text of this book is set in Horley Old Style MT Std.

The Library of Congress Cataloging-in-Publication data is available:
LCCN: 2012954515

ISBN: 978-0-547-76348-4 hardcover
ISBN: 978-0-544-34069-5 paperback

Manufactured in U.S.A.
DOC 10 9 8 7 6 5 4 3 2 1
4500512765

For my mom, Joanne Urban,
who held the stars in place

The connections we make
in the course of a life —
maybe that's what heaven is.
—Fred Rogers

The Beginning

◉ ◉ ◉

In the beginning, there was the donut.

At first, the donut was without form — a shapeless blob of dough, fried in fat of one sort or another. The Ancient Greeks ate them. The Mayans. Even the Vikings enjoyed a platter of puffy dough blobs between pillages.

Miss Leticia Chestnut was not a Viking, but hers was an old recipe, and it became legend in southern New Hampshire for both its extraordinary flavor and its tidy, saucerlike shape. A passing sea captain, Cornelius Bunning, heard tell of her wares and upon tasting them offered Miss Chestnut various riches in exchange for the recipe. When she refused to part with it, he married her, keeping his riches and taking her on as cook aboard his ship, *Evangeline*, where she made her famous donuts every morning.

This included the morning of June 28, 1847, the day that Captain Bunning turned *Evangeline* south into a small headwind, which itself turned into a terrifying gale. He had just been handed his plate of morning donuts when the wind turned treacherous. Thinking quickly, the captain grabbed his donuts one by one and rammed them down onto the spokes of the ship's wheel, thereby preventing them from plummeting to the deck and rolling away.

The storm raged for hours, and Captain Bunning battled it, wind howling, rain lashing. He never lost faith, nor stamina, for Mrs. Bunning's donuts kept him strong.

Upon returning to port, Captain Bunning was met by gazetteers eager to print up his story of bravery in the face of the storm, and Bunning, who enjoyed being the center of all this attention, told the tale in vivid detail — right down to the spokes through his donuts.

The donut may be timeless, but on June 28, 1847, Captain Cornelius Bunning had invented the hole.

Ruby Pepperdine has heard this story at least five hundred times. This is not an exaggeration.

She has heard it twice on the radio just this morning. Of course, it is Bunning Day, and Ruby has been up for hours, folding tissue-paper flowers like Gigi taught her. She has been listening to WNHB as her parents make their phone calls, just as they do every year, to remind her uncles and aunts and driving-aged cousins that they need to be at Pepperdine Motors by noon in order to make it to the parade in time for check-in.

This year, for the first time, Ruby has a place to be too, though she does not need to be in it until one thirty.

It won't be hard to find. A two-foot square has been taped to the sidewalk of Cornelius Circle near the intersection of Main Street. Earlier this morning, Patsy Whelk, assistant Bunning Day Parade coordinator, had stared uncomfortably at the straight lines of the tape and then squatted to draw a chalk circle inside the square, which seemed to her to be more in keeping with the day.

The circle will already be smudged by the time Ruby arrives with Aunt Rachel and Ruby's cousins, Willow (six) and Carter-Ann (three and a half) and Baby Amelia (seven months), but the words inside the circle will be easy enough to make out: ESSAY GIRL.

That's Ruby. This year's Bunning Day Essay Girl.

She has made her wish.

Her time is coming around.

She will stand in her circle—her hole in the center of the taped square—and wait for it.

The Center of Everything

◉ ◉ ◉

If you were from someplace other than this particular part of New Hampshire and were driving through Bunning on your way to Canada or to Santa's Village in Jefferson or simply to take in the autumn foliage, you might not even notice Pepperdine Motors. Actually, unless you were in the market for a great deal on a new or used vehicle, Pepperdine Motors probably would not be of much interest to you.

It was of great interest to Ruby Pepperdine, however. Not for the low, low prices, or for the box of Delish donuts in the waiting room, or for the twice-yearly Moonlight Madness Sale. Pepperdine

Motors was of great interest to Ruby Pepperdine because the roof was flat. And on Sunday nights, after Gigi closed the repair shop and Dad closed the show room and Aunt Lois closed the office, Gigi would turn off the big fluorescent lights that flooded the car lot and she and Ruby would climb the staircase to the roof and they would look at the stars.

"That's Orion," Gigi said one wintry night. "Three stars in a line, that's his belt. See him, Ruby?"

Ruby was little back then, and the sky had looked like one big sheet of stars to her. It wasn't until her grandma Gigi wrapped an arm around her and pointed and Ruby's eyes followed the line of that arm to Gigi's mittened fingertip and out beyond that Ruby found those particular stars in the sky and drew the invisible connections between them.

The next week Gigi's arm pointed out the same constellation, the tip of her mitten one small degree west of where it had been the last time. The next week it was a little farther west and then a little farther, until Orion and his belt and all the neighboring constellations had made their slow march across the sky and out of sight, and others had come to take their place.

If you were Ruby Pepperdine, you might have wondered why that was. Why the sky moved the way it did. And because you were with Gigi, you would ask.

And Gigi would fold both arms around you and explain about orbits and rotations and black holes and the cosmos. She would tell you about big things, bigger than anything you could really understand well enough to explain to your best friend, Lucy, the next day—but while she was telling you, you would have understood it. And while she was saying that the earth moved around the sun, which was itself a star moving around in a dizzying, centerless space, you would have been able to believe it.

And to believe the opposite.

That the center of everything was right here in Bunning, on top of Pepperdine Motors, safe in the circle of Gigi's hug.

Destiny

◉

"Your grandma would have been so proud of you," Aunt Rachel says. She is brushing powdered sugar out of Carter-Ann's hair, but she is talking to Ruby. "Like George Washington's wig." That she says to Carter-Ann. Some people get confused by the way Aunt Rachel slides in and out of talking to her kids and talking to the people in front of her. Grocery clerks, especially. But Ruby is always able to figure it out.

"Thanks." Ruby grins at her aunt. Normally, Ruby would help Aunt Rachel with Carter-Ann, but to do so now would mean stepping out of the chalk circle. Staying in the circle seems like part of the magic. Like this is where fate or the Universe or Captain Bunning will find her. Like this is the spot she's supposed to be in for her wish to come true.

All around her, people are claiming their own spots along Cornelius Circle, clanking open folding chairs and setting down coolers. Some moms fold blankets over the edge of the curb, where they hope their kids will sit for the duration of the parade, even though year after year those same kids can't help but leap to their feet the moment they hear the far-off *whoop-whoop* of Officer Imus's patrol car. Often people toss candy from the floats, and the kids want to be ready. Ruby gets that. She wants to be ready too.

"Willow, use your napkin. Don't give the baby any more donut, Carter-Ann." Aunt Rachel has switched to dusting sugar off the head of Baby Amelia. "You know how Gigi loved this parade."

"I remember," Ruby says. Gigi was the only

grown-up Pepperdine who didn't drive a Pepperdine Motors convertible in the parade. She had too many other places she belonged. Some years she sang with the Sweet Adelines, and others she joined the Planetary Society's Night Owls, all wearing their enormous star costumes, forming constellations as they walked the route. When Gigi was on the city council, she'd had the chance to ride in the back of a Pepperdine Motors convertible, but she marched with Grannies for Groceries instead, handing out flyers about the charity food pantry. Ruby had always loved waving to Gigi as she passed, and having Gigi and all the Night Owls or Grannies or Adelines wave back. It made her feel like she was part of the parade, even if she was only standing to the side of things.

At the funeral home, people had said they could not imagine the Bunning Day Parade without Gigi in it. But here it is. Or here it is about to be.

Across the street from where Ruby is standing, someone has set up a row of milk crates with little pillows on them. That's one of the nice things about

Bunning. You can set up your seats for a parade and go off to get a balloon or a bag of donuts, and nobody will mess with them.

Beyond the crates Ruby can see Memorial Park, which is filled with tall white tents. Many are artists' booths or have kiddie games like Ring Toss and Fish-a-Prize. Some house food vendors: chowder and falafels and hot dogs. The busiest tent is the one Mr. DeNiro sets up for Delish, the local donut shop. When they'd first arrived, Aunt Rachel had left Ruby in the circle in the square while she went there to buy powdered sugar Snow Wonders and chocolate éclairs for the girls.

The real Delish, the store, is on the opposite side of the park. On regular days business is pretty brisk there, but on Bunning Day it is the Delish tent that is really busy — so busy that all the DeNiro kids have to work in it. Derek comes down from Dartmouth to help, and Delilah, who runs track at the high school, works the register, as does her sister, Danielle. Even the youngest DeNiro, who is Ruby's age, has to work. His name is Nero.

"What if the parade doesn't come?" Willow asks.

"It will come, silly pie!" Ruby tells her. "It always comes." She boops Willow's nose with her index cards. Her essay is written on those cards. Ms. Kemp-Davie, the school librarian, had suggested that Ruby use very large printing, and so even though it takes only a minute to read her essay aloud, she has fifteen cards in her hand.

"That says 'tiny.'" Willow's finger, which moments ago had popped the last bit of éclair into her mouth, taps a chocolate swirl onto the top card on Ruby's stack. "Something 'tiny.'"

"Close," says Ruby. She squats down so Willow can see the card better. "It says 'destiny.'"

"What's that?"

"Destiny? It's like fate. Like how things are supposed to happen."

"Let me see!" Willow tugs at the destiny card, and the entire stack flies out of Ruby's hand.

For a moment the world slows down. The

cards hang in midair as Ruby reaches for them. It is almost as if she can read the words —

holes made him famous

tired of drifting around

beams from his beloved Evangeline

— even as the cards bounce off her fingertips and scatter on the sidewalk.

"Oh, Willow!" Aunt Rachel cries.

"It's okay. I've got it," Ruby says, but there are a couple of cards she can't reach without leaving the circle in the square.

That couldn't really mess things up, right? What kind of wish would go flooey just because somebody stepped outside of a chalk circle? Who knows, maybe she is *supposed* to step outside the circle. The truth is, she still hasn't figured all this wish stuff out yet — even though she has spent the past four days trying.

Ruby is careful not to wish that someone would

tell her what she is supposed to do. She has read enough about wishes to know that greedy wishers always have things backfire on them. People end up turning their daughters into gold or getting sausages stuck forever on the ends of their noses. No way will she mess up her real wish by asking for something else.

As much as she'd like to talk to someone about how uncertain she's feeling, she doesn't wish for that, either. Besides, who would listen now? Not Nero, she bets. Certainly not Lucy.

Ruby grabs the last of her index cards and steps back into her chalk circle. Too bad Ms. Kemp-Davie hadn't suggested she number the cards. Okay, which came first? The one about the empty field or the bit about *Evangeline*?

Whoop-whoooOOOooop!

"It *is* coming!" Willow pushes in front of Ruby to stand at the curb. She cannot see the parade yet. No one near the circle in the square can. Officer Imus is still on Elm Street, whooping his siren to

warn people out of the road. It will be two more minutes before he makes a right onto Cornelius Circle,
and another five before he makes his way around
Memorial Park to the spot in front of the circle in
the square. From there he'll continue to Main Street
and turn right again, whoop-whooping for another
mile, until he reaches the rec center, where the parade ends and where the floats will remain on display until after The Hole Shebang—the Bunning
Day fireworks show—that evening.

By then Ruby's wish will have come true. *Everything will be fixed*, she thinks, *and nobody will be
mad, and everything will be back to how it is supposed
to be.* Of course, technically, the wish has until mid-
night to work, but if she has it figured right, things
should happen long before that.

Then again, ever since the day Gigi died, few
things are going like Ruby figures they should.

She shuffles through the cards, searching for
the one that begins her essay—the one with *destiny*
and a chocolate fingerprint.

Some say it was destiny. A brave sea captain, a freak storm, and a platter of puffy dough balls.

Across the street, there are people sitting on the milk crates now: a family of redheads is eating donuts and fanning themselves with parade programs. Beyond them, Ruby can see Nero at the Delish tent. He is tall and skinny, with knobby shoulders that make it look like his T-shirt still has a clothes hanger in it. His dark bangs are tucked up under a Delish cap, and he is clacking a pair of metal tongs like castanets, filling waxed bags with old-fashioneds and crullers and éclairs.

Somewhere near the parade check-in area, Lucy is still fuming—Ruby's pretty sure about that. But Nero doesn't seem upset. He is wearing the same carefree smile that all the DeNiros wear, watching Mr. DeNiro juggle five cider donuts in his plastic-gloved hands.

Maybe Nero has forgotten about yesterday. Maybe he isn't mad after all.

Ruby watches as Mr. DeNiro tosses the donuts one-two-three-four-five high in the air, one after another, and Nero catches them one-two-three-four in a white waxed bag, each donut landing exactly where it is destined to be.

Until, that is, Nero glances in Ruby's direction, and his DeNiro smile slides away. Donut number five drops not into the white waxed bag but at his feet.

Destiny: squirrel food.

The Parade Begins

◉ ⦿ ◉

Twenty yards behind Captain Imus's whooping patrol car, four flag girls from the high school carry a wide banner with blue felt letters that spell out BUNNING DAY. Behind the banner is the rest of the flag squad: six girls in matching sleeveless sweaters and pleated skirts. In November they will wear those sweaters over turtlenecks and wave their flags at football games and wish that they were warmer, but now, in the late-June heat, the girls have lobster-red faces and each is using her own favorite curse word to swear she will never try out for flag again. *Next year,* thinks their captain, Talia O'Hare, *I am joining show choir instead.*

Behind the flag girls marches the school band, playing a nearly recognizable version of "Louie Louie." Behind the band are (in no particular order) eighteen floats, nine Pepperdine Motors convertibles (decorated with Ruby's tissue-paper flowers) carrying a slightly larger number of local dignitaries (undecorated), ten more bands, the Greater Bunning Sweet Adelines, a set of Shriners in tiny cars, thirty-four horses, two Brown Swiss calves, three Scout troops, an array of antique tractors, a shopping cart brigade from the local food co-op, four different daycare groups, two dance schools, one gymnastics studio, a couple of unicyclers, several veterans organizations, Okeda Martial Arts (where Lucy is), the Hungry Nation Youth Theater (where Lucy would have been otherwise), a formation of belly dancers, two magicians, the Bunning Humane Society Dogs of Distinction, a drumming group, the Night Owls, a dozen fire trucks from all over southern New Hampshire, and—near the end of the parade—a replica of Bunning's original one-room schoolhouse, settled on a flatbed trailer and equipped with a powerful sound system.

In years past Ruby would be looking forward to seeing Lucy doing karate moves or watching for whatever group Gigi was marching with. But this year Ruby is thinking about the schoolhouse.

It is the schoolhouse that will stop in front of the circle in the square, in front of the Bunning Day Essay Girl or Boy.

Ruby has seen this happen eleven times— though she only remembers the past five or six. She knows that when the schoolhouse trailer stops, the school librarian, Ms. Olive Kemp-Davie, is supposed to hop out of the pickup truck that tows it, open the schoolhouse window, and turn on the amplification system inside. She will take the microphone out of its case and use it to introduce this year's Essay Boy or Girl, who will step up onto the float and, in 180 words or less, say something about the Legacy of Captain Cornelius Bunning.

Ruby sorts her note cards again.

Some say it was destiny.

She hasn't really read her essay since she printed it on her cards. She was so busy trying to make sure she had things figured out. Now she thinks that maybe she should have practiced a little. How would Lucy read the words?

Some say it was destiny?

Some say *it* was destiny?

Some say it was *destiny*?

Some say it was destiny that Ruby and Lucy became best friends.

They were alphabetical pals in kindergarten. O came before P, so Okeda sat next to Pepperdine at circle time. Destiny.

They stayed friends, too, even when they didn't need to be alphabetical, sitting side by side at lunch and being field-trip buddies and partnering for class projects. They were together so much that teachers sometimes called one Luby and the other Rucy. Neither one minded.

In the summers Ruby would help Lucy learn her lines for whatever Hungry Nation Youth Theater production she was in, and they would stay up late at each other's houses, telling secrets and making plans for what they would do when they grew up (most of which involved moving to New York, where Lucy would be a famous actress and Ruby would be her agent and help her learn her lines).

Ruby knows that if you had somehow met them individually, you wouldn't have pegged them for friends. Probably, you would have guessed Lucy was pals with McKenzie Monk and those girls, because, really, Ruby and Lucy are quite different from each other. Lucy is tall; Ruby is average. Lucy has dark skin; Ruby is pale. Ruby has every-color hair, which means that most people call it brown, the same as her mom's. Lucy's hair is copper colored and curly. Neither of her dads has hair like that. Mr. Okeda's hair is as black and shiny as his lawyer shoes. Mr. Fisch has no hair at all, but there is a picture of him at Lucy's house from when he was a boy. In it his hair is yellow and he is wearing a karate outfit.

Not an outfit, Lucy would say. A *gi*.

Ruby knows that Lucy will be wearing her *gi* today as she walks in the parade with the other students from Okeda Martial Arts. Mr. Fisch always has his students march in the parade, doing kicks and stunts. This year Lucy will be breaking boards—Mr. Fisch will hold them up and Lucy will kick them. She'll get to yell, too. Not *Hi-ya!* like in cartoons. *Kiai!* is what she'll yell. Loud. You have to put your spirit into your words, Lucy says. She knows because she read it on a poster in the Okeda Martial Arts lobby.

Lucy says other poster things too, like "Move and the way will open" and "Mind like water," which is about being calm and having reactions that are appropriate to the circumstances—like if you drop a pebble in a pond, the ripples are the right size for the pebble. Drop a big pebble, you get big ripples. A small pebble, and the ripples are smaller. Mr. Fisch says Lucy is a big rippler. An overreactor.

Ruby is an underreactor, Lucy says. So they are like yin and yang — which are not the names of twin zoo pandas, like Ruby thought at first, but two opposites that fit together.

Lucy is dramatic; Ruby is calm.

Lucy is impulsive; Ruby takes time to figure things out.

Ruby does what she is supposed to do, and Lucy? Well. "I count on you for balance," Lucy always says.

Which is why they are friends, Ruby thinks.

And which is why she hasn't told Lucy how out of balance she has felt since Gigi died. Instead, Ruby pretended things were normal. That she was normal.

And it worked.

Mostly.

Until yesterday.

"We're *supposed* to be best friends!" Lucy had said. Yelled, really. Her eyes had been slits, her voice as loud as it had ever been on the Hungry Nation Youth Theater stage. "I tell you *everything* and you didn't tell *me* anything!"

Ruby's stomach hurts remembering what she had said back. "Mind like water."

"This is not a stupid pebble, Ruby Pepperdine! This is a meteor! You have hurled an enormous *meteor* into the lake of our friendship. You've caused a tsunami!" Lucy had balled her fists and dashed away, and Ruby was left bobbing stupidly in her wake.

Wonders

◉ ◉ ◉

Ruby has to hold Willow's hand to keep her from hopping out into the street. Six years ago, when Ruby was Willow's age, Ruby had been the one hopping, though Aunt Rachel did not have to hold her hand. Even back then Ruby was good at figuring out what she was supposed to do.

In preschool, for example, she figured out that the good kids played in the classroom, and the really bad kids got time-outs and calls home and didn't get to play much at all. But the in-between kids? The ones who were mostly good but might be having a "difficult moment" got to go to the special playroom with the climbing wall and the cushiony floor and the things to swing around on until they cooled off a little. The preschool teachers didn't need you to be perfect—just mostly good. So Ruby had just enough "difficult moments" to get to play in the playroom, but not so many that she'd have to sit in the hall or lose stars from her behavior chart.

In third grade she figured out that if you put your hand up in class when everyone else did, you probably wouldn't get called on, but you also probably wouldn't get called on when nobody put their hand up either. Teachers mostly picked the kids who never put their hands up then, and only once had Ruby been called on when she didn't really want to be. (It was a question about state capitals. It always seemed to her that Detroit should be the capital of Michigan, not whatever it was. Lansing?)

She also figured out how to write a pretty good essay for the Bunning Day Essay Contest. Anybody could've, really. All you had to do was go back and look at the past winners.

First of all, you had to say that Cornelius Bunning was great—brave or smart or an original thinker, it didn't seem to matter which one. And you might mention how glad you were to live in a town named after him—because you wanted to be brave or smart or an original thinker too. It would be good if you could say something funny about donuts. Maybe a pun like they're "holey original" or like "you have a 'hole' lot of opportunity here." You could say "what goes around comes around" or something like that. And your essay had to be about a minute long and the sort of thing people knew to cheer for when it was over. The kind of thing that you could read out loud from the back of a parade float and not bore everybody to death. One hundred and eighty words. That's it.

It is nearly the end of the school year when Ms. Kemp-Davie sets the winning essay down on the stack of travel brochures that always covers her desk in May. It is an anonymous submission like the rest and requires a code key to determine the identity of the writer. The result surprises her, and she has to double check to make sure she has not been distracted by the brochure photos of cruise ships and ancient ruins. But, no, she is correct. The essay belongs to Ruby Pepperdine.

Ruby is a sweet kid and a great reader, but Ms. Kemp-Davie has always thought of her as one of those middle-of-the-pack children, and for a moment she can't help but wish that it was Ruby's friend Lucy who had won the competition. Lucy does theater in the summer, doesn't she? She could have given a dramatic reading at the parade, full of emotion and spirit. Instead, Ruby Pepperdine will probably read her essay like most of the past winners: too fast and too quietly for anyone to hear.

Ms. Kemp-Davie sighs.

It is then that she decides that she is going on that cruise after all. She has been at the Bunning Day Parade twenty-three years in a row. This year, she thinks, snatching up the glossiest of the brochures, they will have to get a substitute. She will be in the Mediterranean.

She is finally going see the Wonders of the Ancient World.

A Long Line of Cars

⊙ ◉ ⊙

The redheaded family is still clapping along to "Louie Louie" when the first of the Pepperdine Motors cars comes into view.

"There's your mom!" Aunt Rachel says, but Ruby is already waving.

Mom waves back quickly and then returns her eyes to the road. Her car carries the mayor, who is sitting up on the trunk of a tissue-paper-flowered premium Mustang convertible, his legs where a passenger's back should be, his feet on the seat.

Ruby never puts her feet on the seat of a Pepperdine Motors car. She sits like her parents expect her to. Feet on the floor mats. Seat belt on.

Dad's car follows Mom's. He's driving three members of the city council, one of whom keeps turning to wave at people on the Delish side of the road and elbowing her fellow councilwoman in the ribs. This is not unintentional.

"Knock 'em dead, Rubes!" Dad calls as he drives past.

Ruby waves her cards at him. "I will!"

After Dad comes Ruby's teenage cousin Fiona and then her cousin Fletcher. Then Uncle Jeff, Uncle Troy, Troy Jr., Aunt Lynn, and finally Uncle David, who wanted to drive the Bunning Day Queen, but Aunt Lynn said he couldn't because he always got too chatty and didn't stay in the center of the road and the spectators got scared half to death thinking he was going to run them over. Aunt Lynn drove the queen. Uncle David got the town manager.

The only other time Ruby Pepperdine has

seen more Pepperdine Motors cars off the lot and all lined up was for Gigi's burial. They drove, single file, from Saint Bart's to Bunning Cemetery in a line so long that Ruby's parents were already parking at the gravesite before the last of the cars — Mrs. Agnes Sigfreid's white Ford Taurus — was pulling out of the Saint Bart's lot.

If you had been standing at the edge of Cemetery Drive, you could have watched them all, all the cars. You could have looked in the windows. Seen the drivers. The passengers. Seen Gigi's old friends in the Pepperdine Motors vans that Troy Jr. and Fletcher drove. You could have seen their sad gray faces. How the ones at the windows peeked up to the sky, through the naked branches, to the places of blue patched between. Seen that their faces had questions on them, but you would not have known if those questions were about Gigi, or about themselves, or about whether the snow just might hold off after all.

You might cry at the cemetery. That would be

okay. Everyone would expect you to cry there. Lucy, in fact, bawled so hard her dads had to take her home.

After that, for a few weeks, you might tear up or sniffle, and that would be okay too. But then Lucy would have moved on to thinking about her upcoming karate tournament, and the city council and the Night Owls and the Adelines and the Grannies would have gone on with their regularly scheduled meetings, and your parents would be back at Pepperdine Motors, working like they always did.

Actually, even more than they always did, since nobody else really understood how Gigi had run the service center and that guy Maurice they had hired was lazy and ate more donuts than the customers, and there was all that legal stuff about how Gigi's ownership shares were to be divided among all her kids and grandkids and even some of the employees who weren't related, which was something Gigi had never talked to them about, that was for sure.

By then everybody else was back to normal. By

then, Ruby figured out, you were not supposed to be so sad.

So she wasn't.

Instead, she went underwater.

That's what it felt like, at least. Every action, every movement, took twice as much effort, as if it were happening in slow motion. Voices sounded farther away, and it took such work to make herself heard that Ruby stayed quiet.

Her family, being so busy, didn't really notice. "You okay?" Lucy had asked a couple of times, but after that she didn't bug Ruby about it. That's the kind of friend she was.

For almost three months Ruby stayed underwater, still doing all the things she was supposed to do. She had to go to Aunt Rachel's after school now, instead of hanging out with Gigi or Lucy, so she helped with her cousins while she was there. At home she did her chores—folding the towels and taking out the kitchen garbage—and did her homework and wrote her Bunning Day Essay. Some things she did a little better than she had before. You can fold towels more neatly if you are slow about it. Write better essays, too, sometimes.

It is possible that Ruby Pepperdine could have stayed underwater forever.

If it hadn't been for Nero DeNiro's color wheel.

Wheels and Spokes

⊙ ◉ ⊙

When you are a sixth-grader at Bunning Elementary, you have Art with Mrs. Tomas, who has you make a color wheel. You can use whatever medium you want: crayons, pastels, paints, colored pencils. Your color wheel can be whatever size you want too. As big as a door or small enough to fit in the palm of your hand. You only have to follow a few rules. You need to include at least twelve colors. You need to keep them in color-wheel order, like a rainbow, with red turning to orange and then to yellow, green, blue, purple. And you need to identify in some way which colors are complementary.

Complementary colors are the ones directly

across the color wheel from each other. Orange and blue, for example. Or purple and yellow.

Ruby's color wheel fit on a regular-size sheet of paper—though the only unlined paper she could find at home was light blue. It didn't matter, though. She did the assignment. She included twelve colors. She used lines—like bicycle spokes—across the middle to show the color complements, exactly like the example on Mrs. Tomas's bulletin board.

Most of her classmates did the same. Some of the wheels were a little messy. A few had clearly been done during indoor recess, when people suddenly remembered the assignment. Lucy had made hers poster-size, nearly big enough to cover the art table.

When Nero sits down next to Lucy, however, it is Ruby's color wheel that he notices. "Blue background, huh? Nice touch."

"Look at this!" says McKenzie Monk, sliding Nero's color wheel over to Ruby.

Ruby had figured out Nero a long time ago. He always did his assignments in a way that nobody else would and asked questions that nobody expected—especially the teachers, who then had to stop whatever lesson they were supposed to be giving and go off on some weird trail that Nero had started. Ruby knows his color wheel will be different, and it is.

He had printed twelve pictures of himself in a T-shirt and pasted them in a circle, like a clock. With markers, Nero had colored in the shirts and added little thought bubbles that showed the complementary colors—with real compliments. "My, Nero. Don't you look dashing in red?" floated above the head of the green-shirted Nero picture. "Hubba hubba. Yellow brings out your eyes!" bubbled up from purple Nero.

Ruby had expected Nero's color wheel to be different, but she did not expect that it would make her laugh. Ruby laughs a real out-loud laugh, which is something you can't do underwater.

When she stops laughing, all the little Nero faces start to blur. And Ruby has a bunch of thoughts.

One of them is that there is something wrong with her eyes.

Another is that there is something wrong with her ears, because when Lucy says, "Are you okay?" it sounds like she's using a speakerphone.

And another is that maybe there is something wrong with her hands, because they have dropped her pencil to the floor, and even though it makes sense for her to bend over and pick the pencil up, her hands are not moving. They are just sitting there on her color wheel, covering up all the complement lines. And there are drops of water landing on her hands and on the painted squares of color, too, and the red and the orange are mixing all up into some other color that Ruby doesn't have a name for and for which there is no complement on her color wheel, and she knows she is going to get a bad grade now.

"Ruby?" That's Mrs. Tomas talking. "Ruby? Did you hurt yourself?"

She did not hurt herself. She hurts, she realizes, but she did not hurt herself.

"Would you like to go see the nurse?" Mrs. Tomas again.

Ruby would not like to see the nurse, but it does seem like she ought not to stay here. Like she should not be crying in Mrs. Tomas's art room and ruining her color wheel.

"Why are you crying?" asks the nurse, whose name Ruby doesn't know. She is just the nurse.

"I don't know," says Ruby. As she says it, she realizes that there is only one thing she could be crying about, and that is Gigi. But she hadn't been thinking of Gigi. She was just looking at Nero's color wheel and then . . .

"Are you sad?" asks the nurse.

Gigi being dead is a sad thing, and thinking about it now makes Ruby feel sad—but she wasn't feeling sad when she started crying. Still, Ruby Pepperdine, who is good at figuring things out, understands that this answer will not be useful to the nurse. And so she says yes. She says that she had been thinking of her grandmother, who had died just a few months ago, and that she got sad.

The nurse asks a few more questions, like if she cries a lot and if she feels depressed and if she wants to talk to a counselor, but Ruby says no. All she wants is a few minutes more to cry in and then she wants to go back to Art and see if she can fix her color wheel.

And the nurse smiles and says take all the time you need, and Ruby says thank you. And she takes some time, which is not all she needs but is all it feels like she ought to take.

Later, after school, after Ruby is done helping Aunt Rachel with the girls and has gone home for supper, and done her homework, and taken out the kitchen garbage, she pulls her color wheel out of her back-pack to see if she can fix it.

The color wheel is really two circles — an out-side circle and a smaller inside circle. Like a car tire. Or a donut. She traces the circumference of each with her finger. Then she traces the complementary color lines, following red to green, orange to blue. All the way across. Diameter.

The lines all meet in the center and spoke out from there. *That's radius,* Ruby thinks. *The line that pokes from the center to the edge.*

That is what happened to her today.

She got poked. She was just sitting there looking at Nero DeNiro's color wheel, and she got poked by a memory or a feeling, zipping along a radius line. Poke. Out of nowhere. Or somewhere, another speck of time. Poke. Poke. Poke.

Ruby knows the speck that poked her too. It was the reason she still feels so sad when everyone else has moved on. She had tried to forget about it, but today it reached out and poked her.

And she wishes there was a way she could reach back.

The Statue

◉ ◉ ◉

If you are ever selected Bunning Day Essay Girl — or Boy, for that matter (there have been more boys than girls, though in the past nine years the only boy to receive the honor was Connor Litigen, who later became a star football player and, later still, an accomplished shoplifter) — you stand in the circle in the square on Cornelius Circle across from Bunning Memorial Park. There is a statue in that park. You can see it clearly: Cornelius Bunning dressed in his captain's coat, one hand fixed to the wheel of *Evangeline* (not that there's really an *Evangeline* there, but the wheel is, and you can't help but imagine the rest) and one hand holding aloft a donut, perfectly round against the sky.

People come with folding chairs and blankets and ice chests to claim spots around you. Some pass through your sightline, but you can still keep an eye on the captain if you want. You can watch birds land on the wheel spokes and on the cap he wears tight on his curly bronze head. Squirrels climb up too, holding hunks of donut in their teeth. If you were closer, you could see the squirrels nibbling. If you were closer than that, you could see the details of Captain Bunning's coat. The pipe sticking out of his pocket. The carvings on his buttons. And you might even notice tiny flecks on the donut he holds. Sprinkles, it might look like to you.

Of course, if you were the Essay Girl—or Boy—or any kid in Bunning, you would know that those sprinkles are really failed wishes. You would know that each fleck was made by a quarter. Not just any quarter, but a 2001 quarter or a 2004 quarter or even a 1966 quarter if you are really old—a quarter from the year you were born, a quarter you had put in your pocket and carried to Bunning Circle on your birthday, a quarter you had held in that pocket until your hand was wet with sweat, until you had whispered your wish — your greatest wish — ninety times (a quarter of the number of degrees in a full circle, of course). A quarter you had held between your fingers while you squinted hard at that do-nut and held your breath and aimed and pitched straight like a dart or arced like a softball or spun like a skipping stone . . .

If the quarter went through the hole in Captain Bunning's bronze donut, your wish would come true.

Everybody knows that.

It is hard to whiz a quarter through the two-inch hole of a bronze donut suspended sixteen feet off the ground. Even those with the best aim usually ting their quarter against the donut edge or Captain Bunning's cold metal fingers. And you only get one chance each birthday. You can't stand there flinging quarter after quarter. One quarter, one chance.

Everybody knows that, too.

But if you did it—through luck or skill or fate or whatever—if you did it, your wish would come true before the next Bunning Day was over.

That, Ruby knows, is why she is standing in the circle in the square on Cornelius Circle. Because on her birthday, her twelfth birthday, her quarter had gone through.

Good Days and Bad

◎ ◉ ◎

The car with Uncle David and the town manager
is followed by Grannies for Groceries, who have
joined the Soup's On Food Co-op in their shopping cart brigade. The third cart on the left is being
pushed by Mitzie Oliver, who is wondering why it
is—even in a parade—that she always chooses a
cart with a back wheel that won't turn.

Behind them is a trailer on which are seated the
seventeen members of Bunning's Sweet Adelines.
They are singing "Blackbird," a song by the Beatles,
which Ruby knows because Gigi was a Sweet Adeline and Ruby used to go with her to some of the
practices. Because of the Adelines, Ruby knows a

lot of songs that most kids her age don't, like "Those Lazy Hazy Crazy Days of Summer" and "Sweet Georgia Brown" and this "Blackbird" song, which the ladies call one of their modern numbers even though it is older than Ruby by about thirty years.

At the back of the trailer stands Mrs. Halloway, who volunteers in the hospital gift shop. She braces her broad belly against a safety rail at the edge of the trailer so that as she sings, she is free to form the words with her hands, making signs she taught herself using the YouSign website. Ruby has watched Mrs. Halloway practice this song so many times that she could sign it too, if she wanted. She could make the sign for g and put it by her mouth, opening and closing her fingers like a beak. That's *bird*. Or arc one hand down over the other. That's *night*.

Ruby's favorite part is when the Adelines sing about the bird flying away. Mrs. Halloway makes the love sign with her right hand and then pushes it up and away into the air, sort of like an airplane.

Sometimes, when Ruby went to visit Gigi in the hospital, she would see Mrs. Halloway at the gift shop. The adults would want to talk about something private, and they'd send Ruby down to the shop with a ten-dollar bill and a list of sodas to buy. Ruby would look around the shop at the get-well-soon stuffed animals and the racks of crossword puzzles and magazines. Because it was December, there were lots of Santas and snowmen and plush red Christmas stockings, too, and a huge box of candy canes marked fifty percent off. There was a wind-up penguin that waddled in a circle, and every time she visited the shop, Ruby wound him up and watched him waddle until he fell over. Then she'd get the sodas and take them to the register.

The Pepperdines didn't want anyone but family seeing Gigi the way she was. Not friends, not co-workers, not even Lucy. So on the days Mrs. Halloway was at the gift shop, she would ask about Gigi, and Ruby would say what she knew she was supposed to say: that Gigi was having a good day or a bad day. That was all.

Ruby did not say that Gigi sometimes woke up with her eyes wild, demanding a pencil, babbling about how she understood and get the pencil get the pencil get the pencil NOW. How once she had the pencil, she would tell everyone to shut up and she would scribble out the shapes that made no sense to anyone else and say, "Don't you see? Don't you see?" And how Ruby would want to see, but how Mom or Uncle David or someone would say, "It's okay, Gigi. It's the medicine you're on. It's just the medicine messing with your head," while someone else would dash to the nurses' station, and pretty soon a nurse would come and give Gigi something that would make her sleep again.

Ruby knew she wasn't supposed to say that. Good day. Bad day. That was all.

Once, on a bad day, Mrs. Halloway had come around from behind the counter to give Ruby a hug. She had a rolling sort of walk that was a lot like the wind-up penguin's, except slower, and each step seemed to take a great deal of planning as well as effort. But today, standing on the back of the Adelines' trailer, Mrs. Halloway looks nothing like a penguin. She stands solid and steady and graceful.

A good day for Mrs. Halloway.

Ruby waves as the Adelines pass, but Mrs. Halloway doesn't seem to recognize her outside the hospital or without Gigi beside her. Her hands are too busy to wave back, anyway. They are making that love sign again. They are pushing away from Mrs. Halloway's chest. They are aiming up toward the sky.

Serious Wishes

◉ ◉ ◉

"May I have your attention, please?" Lucy calls as she steps up onto the lunchroom seat next to Ruby's. She pulls a shiny red kazoo from her pocket and blows a loud, buzzy fanfare. The noisy lunchroom is suddenly quiet.

"Today, May twenty-first," Lucy says in her best stage voice, "is the twelfth birthday of my best friend, Ruby G. Pepperdine." With a flourish, McKenzie Monk pulls a candle from her lunch bag and pushes it deep into Ruby's grilled cheese sandwich. A lunch monitor appears with a book of matches to light it.

Ruby is amazed. "You're crazy," she says to Lucy. For Lucy's birthday last summer, Gigi had taken them both to the movies. There is no way Ruby would have stood up in the theater and kazooed about it.

Lucy grins, then puts on an old-time schoolmarm voice and shushes Ruby with convincing seriousness.

"If you would all please join me in singing 'Happy Birthday'!" She kazoos another note, and just like that, the entire lunchroom is singing — even the cool kids, even the fourth grade boys, even Nero and the kids who don't know Ruby well — all of them are singing "Happy Birthday" and calling her Dear Ruby, and for as long as the song takes, Ruby and Lucy are the center of attention. Then the song ends and Lucy hops down off the seat and the rest of the school goes back to eating or talking or whatever it was they were doing before.

"Ta-daaaaaa!" Lucy sings.

Ruby laughs and blows out her birthday

candle. "That was brilliant," she says. "We're going to have to add 'Master Kazoodler' to your résumé before your next audition."

"Do not mock my talent," says Lucy, tucking the kazoo back into her pocket.

"I'm your future agent. I would never mock you."

"Good. Now the important stuff." Lucy leans in conspiratorially. "What did you wish for?"

Oh, no. She forgot to wish. "All the singing and kazooing and the surprise." Ruby shakes her head. "I can't believe I missed my wish."

Lucy plucks the candle from Ruby's sandwich and licks the melted cheese off it. "It's okay, Rube. You can wish on your birthday cake tonight, right?"

"My dad has a big sales meeting," Ruby says. "We celebrated this morning with birthday donuts."

It had been nice, the three of them sitting down to breakfast together. They had all turned off their phones and eaten donuts, and her parents had kissed her and given her a Katherine Paterson book as a gift. They had said happy birthday and even driven her to school instead of making her wait at the bus stop. But there had not been any candles on her donuts, and she had not made a wish.

And this year, for the first time in twelve years, Ruby had something really important to wish for. Not that her hair would turn curly or that she'd get a new bike or that she'd be better at soccer, but something really, truly important. Something she hasn't stopped thinking about since she saw Nero's color wheel last week. And now she has missed her chance.

"There's always Captain Bunning," says a voice from another table. It is Nero DeNiro.

"Geez, Nero. Eavesdrop much?" Lucy rolls her eyes.

"Once a person kazoos in the lunchroom, she's lost her right to privacy," Nero says. "It's the fate of all celebrities."

Ruby can tell that Lucy would like to stay irritated at him, but she's too flattered by being called a celebrity.

"You *could* try Captain Bunning," Lucy

whispers, once Nero turns back to talking with the boys at his table.

Lucy means the statue in town. She means Ruby can try tossing a quarter and wishing, like that old town legend says. But after school Ruby is supposed to go to Okeda Martial Arts to help Lucy dust and vacuum the lobby (Mr. Fisch has promised to give them five dollars for their trouble), and after that she has to go straight home for dinner with her mom. Besides, she doesn't have a quarter.

Six hours later, however, when Mr. Fisch compliments her dusting and pays Ruby two crisp dollar bills and two round quarters, Lucy cannot help but see that one of those quarters is from their birth year.

"It's fate," Lucy says, hand to her heart. "You are destined to have your wish!"

"You are destined to be a goofball," jokes Ruby, but when she gets a text from her mom saying, **Pick u up?** she texts back, **Walking home.**

The statue of Captain Bunning is not exactly on the way, but it isn't too far out of the way either.

Ruby walks fast.

She holds the quarter in her hand.

She whispers her wish.

She whispers her wish ninety times—exactly like she is supposed to.

Regrets

◉ ⦿ ◉

Ruby doesn't have a ton of regrets. Most of the ones she does have are pretty standard fare. She regrets calling Lucy a turnip once when they were joking around. Some of the other girls overheard and started calling her "Turnip" too. Lucy had gotten crazy mad and didn't talk to Ruby for three days. When she finally cooled down, they both said they were sorry and that was that, but Ruby still regrets saying it in the first place.

What Ruby Pepperdine most regrets, though, is something she cannot say sorry about.

What Ruby Pepperdine most regrets is that she didn't listen.

She didn't listen to Gigi.

Gigi, who would pause a movie right in the middle to explain about history or geography or old-time sayings so that Ruby wouldn't miss anything. Who had taken her to sing with the Adelines and meet with the city council and stare at the stars with the Night Owls. Who had taught her about zoning laws and four-part harmony and the orbit of the planets. Ruby had listened to everything Gigi had ever said to her—even about black holes and dark matter and things so big she could not understand them.

But on that one day, Ruby did not listen.

Gigi had two weeks, the doctor had said. Two months if they were lucky. There was nothing more the hospital could do. So Gigi came to Ruby's house to die.

Dad put a hospital bed in the living room for her, but Gigi wouldn't lie down in it so they wheeled an oxygen tank over to the recliner. They let her stay in the chair, let her doze as she wanted, while the aunts and uncles took turns watching her.

*   *   *

Aunt Lois had taken the overnight shift and gone home. Dad had kissed Gigi on the cheek and took off for Pepperdine Motors—"Somebody's got to hold down the fort." It was Mom's turn to be with Gigi. "I'm just going to jump in the shower, Ruby," she said. "I'll be out in five minutes and then you can go to the bus stop."

Ruby had looked over at her grandmother. She was asleep in her chair, her oxygen tank humming beside her. "Okay," Ruby said.

For a minute or two she sat at the kitchen table and looked at the person in the chair. The person was Gigi, but that was almost as hard to believe as it was to believe in dark matter. Gigi had hair long enough to braid and strong hands that always seemed to be holding something—a wrench or a pencil or a telescope or Ruby's hand.

This person in the chair wore a knit cap over a bald, veined head. Her hands were open and empty, one on the arm of the chair, the other turned up in her lap, like she was waiting for something to drop into it.

Ruby pulled *Concepts in Mathematics* out of her backpack and opened it to last night's homework. Circumference: the distance around. Diameter: cutting across. Radius: the halfway point, poking from the center to the edge.

"Listen."

The person in the chair—Gigi—was awake. Her hand was extended, her eyes wild. "Listen," she said.

Ruby didn't move. "Mom will be right back. She's taking a—"

Gigi pushed against the arms of the chair, struggled to stand up.

"No." Ruby rushed over just like she had seen her mom and dad and aunts and uncles do. Gigi was trying to say something wild and confusing, like at the hospital. "It's the medicine," Ruby said, just like she had heard her parents say. Just like she was supposed to say. "It gives you the dreams. It makes you—"

The bony hand smacked the arm of the chair once. Twice. "Listen." The voice was wilder, louder. "It's all coming together." In between the words there was a gasping sound —"It's all (*gasp*) coming (*gasp*)—"

Ruby kept saying the things that she had heard her family say. "It's the medicine. It's not real. It's nothing to worry about. It's not—"

"Listen," gasped the voice.

And then Mom was there, stepping in front of Ruby and kneeling at Gigi's feet, holding her hand.

"No," Ruby said again. That's when Mom turned to her. "Ruby, go to your bus stop. Go to school. I'll take care of this."

Ruby remembers walking backwards to the kitchen. Seeing Gigi slump back in her chair. Her eyes were still open, but they had lost their wild look. They just looked tired now. Right away Ruby knew something was wrong—that she had done the wrong thing. She remembers wanting to go back to the recliner, to apologize, to listen to whatever it was that Gigi had wanted to tell her.

But Mom had said to go to the bus stop, and so Ruby did. She gathered her homework and put it in her backpack. She put on her boots and her coat and her mittens and her hat, and she went to the bus stop, just like she was supposed to do. She went to school, and she did what she was supposed to do there, too, though all the while she could not help thinking that when she got home she'd try again. She'd ask Gigi what it was she wanted to say. She would listen.

They could have called her at school to tell her, but they didn't. They let her come home on the bus. All those cars in the driveway. PEPPERDINE MOTORS, PEPPERDINE MOTORS, PEPPERDINE MOTORS on every plate. Nobody had to tell her what had happened. Ruby figured it out.

Ruby Will Be Fine

◎ ◉ ◎

There is a tap on Ruby's shoulder. "You're the Essay Girl?" It is Patsy Whelk, assistant coordinator of the Bunning Day Parade. She has a clipboard that she taps in time with "Amazing Grace," which is being played now by the Graniteers Regional Pipe Band.

"That's me." Ruby holds up her index cards as proof. The heat of her hands has warped them, and they curve like the sail of a ship.

Patsy Whelk nods and presses a button on the headset she is wearing. "Got her," she says into it. Then she looks back at Ruby. "You all set? You know what you're supposed to do?"

"She knows," Aunt Rachel says.

"No no no no no no!" Carter-Ann does not like the bagpipes.

"Cover your ears, sweetie. Sweetie? Cover your ears. They'll be gone in a minute," Aunt Rachel says.

"Okay. Couple of things. Speak clearly into the mike." Patsy Whelk taps her clipboard. *That saved* — tap — *a wretch* — tap — *like me* — "Got a phone on you, turn it off. Don't want someone trying to talk to you while you're up there." Tap, tap, tap.

Yes, I do, Ruby thinks as she pulls her phone from her pocket and turns it off.

"All right, then. Any questions? You set?"

"I have to get my cards in the right order." She has been so busy watching the parade and, well, thinking about things, she has almost forgotten about her speech.

"Get them ready. Don't want to mess this up." Patsy Whelk taps twice more on her clipboard. "I'll be back," she says, and then she disappears into the crowd.

"Ruby will be fine," Aunt Rachel says to the spot where Patsy Whelk used to be. "She always is. Aren't you?"

Ruby smiles for Aunt Rachel.

"They're going, honey. Look. See?" The bagpipers' backs are to the circle in the square now, their kilts swishing side to side with every step. Carter-Ann lifts one hand from her ear and then smooshes it back down. They might be going, but she can still hear their music.

Ruby sorts through her cards. Patsy Whelk is right. She should not be thinking about Nero or Lucy or anything else. She should be thinking about not messing up. Okay, the destiny card is first, but what comes next? Ruby finds the card near the back of the stack and slips it in where it belongs.

Donut holes made him famous, but being a sailor was what Captain Bunning loved. When he and his ship grew too old to sail,

How Ruby Knew

◉ ◉ ◉

If you are a sixth-grader at Bunning Elementary, the last three weeks of school are likely to be so busy that you might not even tell your best friend about your quarter sailing through Captain Bunning's bronze donut. She might be busy with her auditions for this summer's Hungry Nation play, and you might not want to distract her. And if you did tell her about the quarter, she'd ask what you wished for. And you'd have to tell about the day Gigi died. About messing everything up. And how maybe you aren't as good at figuring things out as you're supposed to be.

Besides, you might not be entirely sure your wish is going to come true.

You might have messed up the wishing, too. Maybe you miscounted and said your wish eighty-nine times or ninety-one times instead of the exact right ninety. You have no proof that a wish is in the works. Nothing felt different after your quarter went through the donut. Nothing, as far as you can tell, has changed.

So you don't say anything. You focus on the end of the year. There are tests to take, after all, and final projects to present and desks to clean out and assemblies to attend. The kindergarteners will host a "Goodbye, Sixth-Graders" picnic, and you will eat egg salad sandwiches and try to remember what it felt like to be six and have your whole life ahead of you.

There will be a field trip to the middle school, where you'll tour the classrooms and the hallways and meet the school principal and the counselors and a librarian who seems nice but who tells you this is her last week of school too. That she is retiring in order to spend more time showing her champion corgis. And you will try not to stare at the middle school students, who look so much older and taller and bigger and cooler. You will wonder if they remember what it feels like to have just turned twelve.

And then it will be time for graduation. There's a ceremony a few days before the rest of the school lets out, and if you are a girl like Ruby Pepperdine, you will sit in a folding chair up on the stage with your classmates and look out at all the parents and grandparents and uncles and aunts. Speeches will be made about your past and your future, and your teachers will hand out awards. Outstanding Student in Mathematics. Outstanding Student in Language Arts. Outstanding Musician.

Your student council leaders, McKenzie Monk and Mark Davis, will announce awards voted on by your classmates: Funniest. Friendliest. Most Dramatic (which goes to your best friend, Lucy). Most

Likely to Succeed (which goes to McKenzie Monk and Mark Davis).

If you were Ruby Pepperdine and knew that none of these awards was going to be given to you, you might find yourself thinking about something else, like how your family would be going out to dinner that night or about the tiny hole you just discovered in the pocket of your dress. Or, more likely, you'd be looking out at your parents and thinking how weird it is that Gigi isn't here with them. How weird everything is now that Gigi is not here. You might even get that poke, poke, poke feeling just as Bunning Elementary School librarian Ms. Kemp-Davie steps up to the microphone to announce the Bunning Day Essay winner.

And even though you are very good at figuring things out, you would not expect to hear your name and could not be more surprised if Captain Bunning himself had made the announcement. Which might make you think that maybe he did. Or that he had something to do with it, at least.

And then you would know it, as sure as you know Orion's Belt. The reason you have been selected as the Bunning Day Essay Girl is not because your essay is so great.

It is because of your wish.

This is the way that your wish will come true.

Ruby's Dream

◎ ◉ ◎

It goes like this:

Ruby is alone on the roof of Pepperdine Motors.

Above her are the constellations, but instead of resting still and quiet in the night sky, they zip about like kids on a playground. Taurus and Leo chase each other in circles. The Big and Little Dippers cross handles like swords.

Orion is absent.

Ruby knows, in the dream, that it is her job to sort them out, to stop their wild swirling.

"Stop!" she commands the stars. "Go back!" The stars don't listen.

Finally, she spots a wayward Cancer. She raises her hand to catch his claw, and as she does, her feet lift off the rooftop. She rises higher and higher into the night. She drifts, lost and alone in the dizzying blackness.

Wishes and Work

⊙ ◉ ⊙

Four nights in a row Ruby has the dream. Four mornings she wakes with the unsettled feeling of not-yet-finished homework.

Being Essay Girl is the first step toward her wish coming true, she is sure of that. But on the fourth morning she can't help but wonder. What if her dream is trying to tell her something? What if there is something more she is supposed to do?

In most of the books that Ruby has read, people stumble upon a genie or an enchanted fish and—*poof!*—their wish is granted. But every once in a while there is a story in which a wish can't happen until the wisher accomplishes certain tasks.

Puts in a little elbow grease. Maybe he has to figure out that the coin he is holding will give him only half of what he wishes for, or he needs to solve a riddle before things kick into motion.

What if a Captain Bunning wish is an elbow-grease wish?

She can't know for sure, but Ruby Pepperdine is a strong believer in extra credit. It can't hurt to try. And so, as she sits down to eat her breakfast in front of the laptop her parents keep in the kitchen, she begins to look for signs that will tell her what else, if anything, she needs to do.

It seems like a good idea to start with Captain Bunning. Between bites of cereal, Ruby searches the Bunning Historical Society website. There are whole pages on Captain Bunning, of course, but the word *wish* does not appear on any of them. The word *donut* appears a lot.

"Are you still here?"

Ruby jumps in her seat. Cheerios and milk splash onto the floor. "Mom!" Ruby says. "You scared me!"

"Just a second, Lois," Mom says into her cell. "I'm sorry, honey. I thought your dad took you to Rachel's already." She grabs a roll of paper towels. "Lois? Hold on. I just have to—"

"I got it." Ruby takes the towels from her mom, who mouths a silent *thank you*.

"Okay, Lois, what did Maurice do now?" Mom steps back into the living room while Ruby wipes the milk up off the kitchen floor. "A week's worth of headaches—and it's only Tuesday," her mother says.

Ruby drops the soggy paper towel in the trash can and returns to the laptop. Instead of the Bunning Historical Society site, the screen now shows an enormous cruller and the words *Giving the Donut Its Due: A Blog of Donut History and Culture*. She must have accidentally clicked on something when her mom startled her, Ruby thinks, and she is about to click back when another thought occurs to her: What if she is *supposed* to read this page?

What if destiny made her click on it and there

is something on this blog that she is supposed to know?

Ruby skims the History of Donuts page. Greeks. Mayans. Vikings. There is one sentence about Captain Bunning. She reads about donut ingredients and donut dunking, and then she sees something that surprises her. It is a description of donut shapes.

Donuts have always been circles to Ruby. In preschool, when they learned about shapes, pizza slices illustrated what a triangle was and sandwiches were squares. Rectangles were chocolate bars and ice cream sandwiches. A donut was always a circle.

But *Giving the Donut Its Due* says the donut — the round kind with a Captain Bunning–style hole in the middle — is not a circle. It is a torus. A three-dimensional shape. Like a ring. Like a tire.

A tire is like a wheel, Ruby thinks.

And a wheel sometimes has spokes. Like radius.

What if *this* is her sign?

Mom paces back into the kitchen, the phone still up to her ear. "I'll be there as soon as I can," she says. Ruby can hear the whine of Aunt Lois's reply, though the only words she can make out are "Maurice" and "exhaust pipe." Mom rolls her eyes. "Lois? Lois. I'll be—I just have to take Ruby—"

"It's okay, Mom," Ruby says. "I can walk." It's not a long walk, really. And she can use the quiet to think.

"You don't mind? And you're going to Lucy's this afternoon, right?"

"To her rehearsal. And then back to Aunt Rachel's. And then home."

"You, Ruby Pepperdine, are an angel." Mom glances at the kitchen clock. "Okay, Lois. I'm on my way. I know. I know. We're running out of time."

Ruby shuts down the computer and grabs her backpack. She is running out of time too. Bunning Day is on Saturday. It has taken her twelve years to learn that a donut is not a circle. How is she to figure out what else, if anything, she is supposed to do about her wish in only four days?

Inner Gretel

◦ ◉ ◦

When the Happy Days preschoolers began the parade a half hour ago, most sported tiny toy drums that they proudly beat in unison. By the time they reach the circle in the square, however, there is little united about them. Many have handed off their drums to parent volunteers, and several more have given up marching entirely, happy to be pulled along in wagons. One of them, Titus Finch, is pretending he is in the Indianapolis 500, which is difficult to do when the person pulling you refuses to run. Still, Titus makes engine noises and from time to time contents himself by squealing around imaginary curves.

His Inner NASCAR Driver, Ruby thinks. That's what Lucy would say.

Lucy had explained it the other day as they walked to her first *Hansel and Gretel* rehearsal. "It's like I believe so much that I'm Gretel that when I see my reflection, I really expect to see a German girl in pigtails and a dirndl. That's a skirt."

Ruby knew what a dirndl was. Gigi had one. It was her only skirt. Mostly she wore pants.

"During a performance, it's an even stronger feeling," Lucy went on. "Like last year, when I was Cinderella's stepsister? I totally *was* that stepsister. It was like there was just enough Lucy left to keep me from crashing off the edge of the stage when I was pretending to leave a room."

"Is it scary?" Ruby had asked.

"It's a little scary right before I go on, but when I'm onstage and everyone's watching, that totally goes away."

Lucy meant that performing was not scary, but that was not Ruby's question. "Is it scary not to be yourself?"

This made Lucy laugh. "It's not like some alien comes out of nowhere and takes over your body. It's that there's this stepsister inside of you, but you don't even know it until you need her."

"You think I have an Inner Stepsister?"

"Not *you*, goofball. Me. *My* Inner Stepsister. *An actor's* Inner Stepsister."

"You think I *don't* have an Inner Stepsister, then?"

Lucy had looked at Ruby like an easy-peasy math problem — the kind you're grateful to see on a test. "You are Ruby Pepperdine, through and through," she said, wrapping her arms around her friend. "That is why we love you!"

Carter-Ann waves at Titus Finch, who is now roaring down an imaginary straightaway, headed for the checkered flag. "That boy's a racer!"

"He sure is," Ruby says, tugging one of her cousin's curls.

Willow corrects them both. "He's just a kid. Real-life racers have helmets."

That is why we love you, Lucy had said. Because she was Ruby Pepperdine *through and through.* But what if she wasn't the Ruby they knew? What if Lucy and Aunt Rachel and everybody else found out she had an Inner Ruby who had totally messed up? Then what would they think of her?

What You Need
to Understand

◎ ⦿ ◎

When her parents are at Pepperdine Motors, Ruby goes to Aunt Rachel's to help out with the girls. Aunt Rachel keeps a laptop on a desk in the living room, and sometimes Ruby uses it to play games. Willow usually watches, and sometimes Carter-Ann does too. *How come that guy with the mustache won't let you get the banana?* Carter-Ann might say, and Ruby will explain. *Well, how come you can't touch the oranges?* Willow will ask, and Ruby will explain that, too. All through the game, questions and explanations. It keeps her cousins out of Aunt Rachel's hair, but it is not the best way to win a game.

It turns out that it is not the best way to learn about a torus, either.

"That's a donut." Carter-Ann points to a drawing on the computer. Ruby has opened a wiki page, and the screen is covered in blue things and red things and long definitions and a few diagrams, like the one that Carter-Ann has spotted.

"An old-fashioned," Willow says in the know-it-all voice that Carter-Ann hates. "The kind that tastes like cake."

"Actually, it's a torus," Ruby says.

"Does it taste like cake?" Carter-Ann asks.

"It's a shape. It doesn't taste like anything."

Carter-Ann folds her arms in disgust. "It should. Everything should taste like something."

"Air doesn't taste like anything," says Willow.

"It does too," snaps Carter-Ann. "It tastes like snow."

"Does not!" says Willow.

Carter-Ann reasserts that it does too, and Willow counters with her belief that it does not. This continues long enough for Ruby to read the torus definition on the screen. She reads that the plural of *torus* is actually *tori*, and that tori look like donuts or tires, which she already knows. She also reads that a torus is a topological space, and has to click on *topological* to find out what that is.

Topological has a lot of definitions, one of which is "the study of a given place, especially its history as indicated by its topography." This is not particularly helpful.

Another definition, a mathematical one, says: "The study of properties of geometric figures or solids that are not changed by homeomorphisms, such as stretching or bending." Ruby is tempted to find out what *homeomorphisms* are but decides that all this clicking is distracting her from the task at hand, and returns to the torus page.

"I want pictures," says Carter-Ann, squeezing into Ruby's lap. "That's just words. I can't read words."

"I can," boasts Willow. "There's a *the* and

there's a *the* and that's *the,* too. Go downer, Ruby, so I can find another *the.*"

"You guys, I need to concentrate," Ruby says, but Carter-Ann is pushing the DOWN key, sending the words scrolling past. Willow yanks Carter-Ann's hand from the keyboard, and the screen goes still again.

"What's that?" asks Carter-Ann, pointing.

The screen is covered in long formulas with squiggles and symbols all over the place. "That's math," Ruby says.

Willow shakes her head. "No, it isn't. That's got letters. Math is numbers."

Ruby likes the kind of math that Mr. Cipielewski teaches. You start with numbers or even a story with some numbers in it, and you do what you're supposed to do and you get the answer, the one right answer. But she has no idea what you're supposed to do with math that looks like this. "It's calculus," she tells her cousins. "Or trigonometry or something."

"See?" Willow says to Carter-Ann. "Not math."

Ruby continues past a few more complicated-looking squiggles until the screen shows some diagrams that look like donuts with webbing on them.

"Look!" squeals Carter-Ann. "A Spider-Man Donut!"

"Spider-Man Donut saves the day!" Willow jumps onto the couch and shoots an imaginary web at her sister.

"Hey! *I'm* Spider-Man Donut," says Carter-Ann.

"Nuh-uh, I am. You're the villain—you're Bran Flakes Man." Willow is not a fan of breakfast cereal.

"*I'm* Spider-Man Donut, right, Ruby? I saw it first!"

Ruby closes the laptop. There is no way she is going to be able to concentrate here. Besides, the stuff on the Internet is so hard. Maybe she could skip Lucy's rehearsal today and go to the library in town. Maybe in the children's room she can find a torus book without such hard math in it.

Who knows? Maybe she is *supposed* to go to the library.

A pillow zings across the room to bonk Ruby on the head. "I webbed you!" Willow hollers.

She is definitely supposed to go to the library.

The Order of Things

◦ ⦿ ◦

It would be possible, if you were standing in the circle in the square or sitting on a cushioned milk crate or resting near the statue of Captain Bunning and wishing you had remembered to bring a hat, not to give a single thought to how this parade came to be.

But a parade doesn't organize itself.

There are volunteers who sell ads for the commemorative program or hand out water bottles at the rec center or decide the order in which the parade entries will march down the route. In Bunning, that last job falls to Patsy Whelk.

Six miles north of the circle in the square is a

small apartment building with four units, one of which is an airy studio rented by Patsy. You might notice the skylight first. Or Patsy's bright orange couch. Or maybe even the framed posters that lean against one another in the foyer, making it difficult for you to actually enter the studio. But once you had made it inside, you could not help but notice the sticky notes that snake along the circumference of Patsy's studio walls. There are eighty-six of them, exactly as many entries as are in this year's Bunning Day Parade. There are blue stickies for the musical acts, and pink ones for the floats. There are purple stickies for each of the town dignitaries, and yellow for the entries that need to be followed by a "pooper patrol."

Over the years, Pasty has learned to space out the bands so their music doesn't clash. She has learned that the cute factor of preschoolers is magnified when they follow a group of senior citizens. People turn thoughtful when the VFW marches by in their uniforms, and even more thoughtful if you put the local Scout troop after that.

She has also learned that she can't always predict what will make folks happy or sad or reverent. While the Night Owls in their constellation formations might make most people smile, others might turn wistful, or even wishful, seeing all those stars.

For weeks Patsy has been arranging and re-arranging the stickies on her wall. She walks slowly along the Post-it parade, imagining how it will look on Bunning Day. Some days she switches a few things, remembering how often bagpipes are played at funerals and how that might not set exactly the right mood for Grannies for Groceries. Or how freaked out the barefoot karate people might be if they have to follow the girls from Kennilworth Stables. She switches. She adjusts. A new parade goes by.

On the day before she is required to turn in the final list, she makes one last change, swapping

Head-Over-Heels Gymnastics and the Bunning Historical Society, moving the latter closer to the schoolhouse float.

Patsy walks the circumference of the apartment.

This is it. This feels right.

This is her parade.

Asking the Right Questions

◦ ◉ ◦

The children's room of the Bunning Free Library has large windows, beanbag chairs, and a cluster of round tables at which, on weekdays, homeschool kids sometimes daydream about passing notes and eating lunches on trays. One of them, Daisy Rangotta, is considering setting up an online business that sells school uniforms and lunch trays and stuff like that—just for homeschool kids like herself.

This being summer, however, there are no homeschoolers at the tables when Ruby arrives. There is a pair of twins attempting to play Connect 4 and a group of intense-looking kids who say things like "Orc-lord" and "hit points" and "You forget,

Panoptocles, that I am a fourth-level mage — prepare to meet your fate."

Was that a sign? That boy saying "fate" when she walked in the room? Maybe she was fated to come to the library today. Maybe this is where she'll really understand tori or homeomorphism or whatever it is that she needs to make her wish work right.

A cardboard grandfather clock on the circulation desk announces that the librarian will be back in fifteen minutes. *That's okay*, Ruby thinks. Torus stuff has to be in either Math or Science, and she can find those sections by herself. Quickly, Ruby heads for the nonfiction section.

"Hey, Ruby Tuesday," says a voice.

"Ruby Tuesday" is the title of an old song she knows from hanging around with the Adelines, but the voice did not sound like it belonged to an Adeline. It sounded like a boy's voice. Ruby peeks around the History shelf to see Nero DeNiro sitting at a small round table.

"Hey," Ruby says back. Dang! She doesn't have time for Nero. Aunt Rachel had said she could go to the library instead of Lucy's rehearsal, but only for a half hour. Still, just saying "Hey" and walking away seems sort of rude.

"*The Seven Wonders of the Ancient World*," she says, peeking at the cover of the book he is reading. There. That wasn't rude. Now Nero can say *Yes* and Ruby can say *That's nice* and then she can move on to the Math section and look for torus stuff.

Instead, Nero shakes his dark hair out of his eyes and makes a raspberry sound. "Says who?"

"What do you mean? Says the author."

The raspberry returns. "She's just writing about the wonders. Somebody else decided to call them that."

Ruby should move on to the math books. She really should. But she can't help but be a little curious. "Who decided?"

"Nobody knows for sure. That's what bugs me. Some medieval guys discovered this list and said it was based on a bunch of other lists from some ancient guys, including . . ." Nero flips to the introduction. "Including a historian dude called Herodotus and another guy named Callimachus, but nobody knows who *really* decided what the Seven Wonders are. So how come we're all supposed to just say, 'Yeah, okay. Those are the Seven Wonders.' What if there was something else around that Callimachus just didn't like? Some kind of awesome tomb or statue or something that was made by one of his enemies, so he left it off the list?"

This is exactly the kind of question that gets Nero DeNiro in so much trouble at school—the kind of question that teachers can't answer. A couple of teachers liked Nero for it. Mr. Cipielewski, in particular, thought Nero's questions showed an active and creative mind, but even he had to keep Nero in line, because otherwise they would never get through all the day's materials, and then when it was time for the assessment tests, it would look like his students hadn't learned anything, even though they had learned many amazing nonassessable things.

"Also," says Nero, "how come nobody gets named Callimachus anymore?"

Ruby can't help laughing. "Would you want to be named Callimachus?"

"I don't want to be named Nero," says Nero. "That's the trouble with names. You don't get to decide your own. Somebody else picks them."

Ruby likes her name. She is Ruby Giselle Pepperdine. The Ruby part has pep and the Giselle has elegance. When she goes to college, she thinks, she might ask people to call her Giselle. Until then, she's fine with Ruby.

"Maybe superheroes," says Nero. "Maybe superheroes get to choose their own names. And villains. I mean, what parent is going to name his kid the Green Goblin?"

"They named him Norman," says Ruby, who saw a lot of superhero movies during Uncle Dave's shifts watching Gigi.

Nero grins. "I never know what to expect from you, Ruby Tuesday."

Is he joking? She and Nero aren't friends or anything, but they have been in class together for three years in a row. Everyone knows what to expect from her. That's why people always pick her to bring notes to the office or to help take care of little kids. They expect her to do what she's supposed to do. Everybody says so. Her parents. All her teachers. Lucy.

"Are you making fun of me?" Ruby asks.

"Blue color-wheel paper. Essay Girl. Norman Goblin. All unexpected," Nero says. "I was giving you a compliment. Now you say thank you."

He is *making fun of me*, Ruby thinks, and she gives him a raspberry, which makes him laugh. "See what I mean?"

There is a ringing sound, like an old-fashioned alarm clock, and Nero pulls a phone from his pocket. "Break's over," he says. "I have to be at Delish with my mom most days, but she lets me play Frisbee in the park or come here for an hour in the afternoon. She says she does not want me gallivanting around town."

Ruby nods. "I guess I understand that."

"You understand that? Ruby, I have never gallivanted. Have you gallivanted?"

"I don't think I'm the gallivanting type," she says.

"Nobody is. It's just a thing that moms say. Why do they say that?"

"I don't know. I've never thought about it before," Ruby admits.

Nero leaves the *Seven Wonders* book on the table but picks up a novel, *The Seven Wonders of Sassafras Springs*, from a YOU MUST READ THIS display. "Maybe I'll see you here tomorrow?"

"I have to do errands with my aunt tomorrow," Ruby says.

Nero shrugs. "Another time," he says as he heads for the circulation desk. The grandfather clock is gone, and Ruby can see that the librarian has returned to her station.

How long has she been talking with Nero? Ruby checks her phone. Dang! He did it. Just like in school, Nero has sucked up all the time she was supposed to be doing something else. Maybe she can come back on Thursday. She has promised Lucy that she won't skip another of her rehearsals

(*I do better knowing you're there,* Lucy had said), but maybe she could come by earlier? Nero wouldn't be here to distract her, and she could focus. She had to focus. By then there would be only two more days until Bunning Day.

B home in 5 minutes, she texts Aunt Rachel. Quickly, Ruby grabs *A Wrinkle in Time* from the YOU MUST READ THIS shelf and checks it out. She arrives at Aunt Rachel's at 4:26 — exactly when Aunt Rachel expected her.

It isn't until 8:12, after Ruby has gone home and eaten dinner and taken a shower and sat down with *A Wrinkle in Time,* that she thinks again about her wish, and that terrible not-yet-finished feeling returns. Thanks to Nero, she is no closer to figuring things out. Was she supposed to understand tori? Or something else?

In the Pepperdine Motors service center, right next to the time clock, Gigi had hung a poster: IF YOU'RE NOT GETTING THE RIGHT ANSWERS, MAYBE YOU'RE NOT ASKING THE RIGHT QUESTIONS.

Ruby has been pretty good at knowing what questions to ask in the past. People didn't sigh when she asked them, or shake their heads, or tell her to stay on topic, like they did with Nero.

But what if wish questions are different? Ruby runs her finger around the edge of the book's award sticker while she thinks. What if figure-out-how-a-wish-works questions are wild, off-topic, spinning-out-of-control questions that she doesn't know how to ask?

And then she understands.

It *was* fate that brought her to the library.

She may not know how to ask those kinds of questions—but Nero DeNiro does.

What Matthew Bennet Wishes

⊙ ◉ ⊙

If Matthew Bennet had known that he would be the only boy his age who was trying out for the play, he would not have done it. He didn't really want to be Hansel. He was thinking maybe he'd be the dad. Or one of those gingerbread kids. But he was loud and a fourth-grader and a boy. So the director said he was Hansel.

Which was kind of okay until he found out that he had to be in the parade, too.

It was like a promotional thing, all the kids from the Hungry Nation Youth Theater walking in the parade and handing out flyers so that people would know about the show. And that was kind of okay too. He had even told a couple of friends that he was going to be in the parade and they could look for him.

That was before he knew about the lederhosen.

Lederhosen are shorts, except not normal shorts. They are dorky green leather shorts and they're scratchy and tight and they have these crazy ladder-looking suspenders with flowers embroidered all over the place. Like the kind an organ grinder's monkey might wear. Only stupider on anyone who is not a monkey. Lederhosen are what Matthew Bennet is wearing as he walks down the middle of Cornelius Circle.

He wishes he had never tried out for the stupid play.

He wishes he had never agreed to be Hansel.

He wishes that there was no such thing as leder-stupid-hosen.

It is not just the lederhosen that look stupid either. His whole costume is stupid. He has on a floofy white shirt and a hat like Peter Pan's—with an actual feather in it. He has on knee socks. Brown knee socks. And brown lace-up shoes, too. He is carrying a fake loaf of bread.

But that's not the worst of it.

The worst of it is all the little kids watching the parade. The ones who can't read yet. Who can't figure out that the words on the banner carried by the gingerbread dancers say HANSEL AND GRETEL AT HUNGRY NATION YOUTH THEATER.

The kids who see gingerbread and think only of Christmas.

"Look!" they say. "It's an elf! It's Santa's elf!"

"I'm not a stupid elf!" Matthew had yelled at the first kid who said it. "I'm a stupid German kid!" But his director had dashed up and told him to be quiet and smile and wave.

He was being quiet now, anyway.

It would be easier if Gretel were here. More people would know they were Hansel and Gretel if they walked together, probably. Even if he and Lucy looked nothing alike. They'd be dressed the right way, and, anyway, Lucy was such a good actor, everybody would know just from looking at her who she was.

It wasn't fair that she got to do karate instead.

He didn't blame her, though. He'd be kicking stuff if he could.

At least he knew his lines. Lucy didn't yet. She was always messing them up onstage. One minute she'd be all Gretel-like, and the next minute her face would crack like one of those boards she was kicking and someone would have to tell her what to say. And then she'd say it six different ways, like she was hoping one of them would stick. But then she'd forget again.

If that happened in front of an audience, it'd be really embarrassing.

Almost as embarrassing, he thinks, *as wearing lederhosen.*

"Hey, elf!" yells a kid.

I'm freakin' HANSEL! Matthew wants to scream. *I've got a stupid fake loaf of bread!* That's it. The next kid who says anything about Santa or what they want for Christmas, he is chucking the loaf at them. He doesn't care.

"It's Santa's elf!" someone squeals.

Matthew tightens his grip on the loaf and looks for the source of the squeal. It is a little girl with chocolate on her face. She is grinning ear to ear. Rats.

And standing behind the chocolate-faced girl is that friend of Lucy's who comes to some of the practices. Double rats.

Matthew sees Lucy's friend bend down to say something to the little girl. "He's Hansel," it looks like. The kid's face changes from a grin to a frown.

"Elf!" she yells at him.

This parade cannot end soon enough.

Another Rehearsal

◦ ◉ ◦

The stage lights are on, but the Hungry Nation auditorium lights are not. Ruby covers her phone so that when she checks the time, the actors won't see its glow. In three minutes Nero should be at the library.

For the past two days Ruby has been thinking that his crazy questions might be the key to figuring out what else she might need to do to make her wish come true. But yesterday she had been stuck helping Aunt Rachel with her errands, and as soon as Ruby woke up this morning, Lucy had called, reminding her about that afternoon's rehearsal.

"I'll be there," Ruby had promised, and she had kept her word. She is here.

Up on the stage, Inner Gretel shivers. "It's getting late," she says.

"But you mustn't go," says the witch. "I have more treats for you inside."

Lucy's Inner Gretel looks cautious, but her pretend brother dashes across the tape line that indicates where the door to the witch's gingerbread house will stand once the tech department has finished painting it.

"Hansel!" Inner Gretel calls. She peers around the imaginary door frame as if she cannot see Matthew Bennet's Inner Hansel standing right there in front of her. A long silence follows.

Ruby checks the time again. Nero is at the library now.

"'Don't go in there,'" the director says in a tired voice. "Lucy, your line is: 'Hansel, don't go in there.'"

Lucy blows out a deep breath. "Sorry. Okay. Hansel, don't go *in* there. Hansel, don't go in *there*."

Ruby should go to the library. Obviously, she

isn't helping Lucy by sitting here. And if she's quick, she can be back before Lucy even notices she's gone.

She finds a flyer for violin lessons on the floor under one of the theater seats and scribbles a note on the back of it, just in case.

Returning library book. Be right back!

When she gets to the library, she spots Nero at one of the round tables, reading intensely.

She shouldn't interrupt him—but Bunning Day is only two days away. This might be her only chance. Ruby picks up a copy of *When You Reach Me* from a nearby display. Okay. If she drops the book, then Nero is bound to look up. If he says hi, then that is a sign that she should go over to his table and talk to him and listen to his questions and—

"Hey, Ruby Tuesday," Nero says.

Dang! She hasn't dropped the book yet! Does that mean that Nero saying hello is *not* a sign? Or that it is such an *important* sign that fate or the Universe or Captain Bunning or whoever is in charge of signs didn't even need her to drop the book to send it?

"Did you like that one?" Nero asks.

"Huh?" Ruby says. It takes her a second to realize what he is talking about. "*When You Reach Me*? It won a Newbery." There is a gold sticker on the front of the book that says so. "This one did too," she says, pulling *A Wrinkle in Time* from her backpack.

"I can see that," says Nero. "But I can't see if you liked them. You have to tell me that part. Or make your own sticker that says so and put that on the book."

Ruby laughs. "That'd be all right," she says, imagining her face on a shiny gold seal. "The Pepperdine Prize."

"So," says Nero, pushing his hand through his hair, "would those books win the Pepperdine Prize?"

In her years as a Bunning Elementary student, Ruby has been asked whether or not she liked a particular book seventy-four times, although she could not tell you this number exactly. What she could tell you is that if you said you liked this part or that part, people would fill in the rest. If they liked the book, they would think you did too. And if they didn't, that you didn't either, and they'd think the one part you mentioned was the *only* part you liked. Most of the time, Ruby figured, people just wanted you to agree with them. And so most of the time she found a way to do so.

But for some reason, Ruby isn't so worried about that with Nero. "Yeah, they'd win a Pepperdine Prize," she says. "Except both those girls — Meg and Miranda — they have this stuff happen to them that doesn't happen in real life. Time and Mrs Which and aliens and all that. Miranda is more regular, but there's still that yelling man and living in New York City."

"People do live in New York City in real life," says Nero.

Ruby knows this, of course. But to her, New York City is the Empire State Building and those lions in front of the library and people selling hot dogs from carts. It seems impossible that kids really live in New York City. That they walk home from school and play soccer with their friends and eat apple crisp, just like kids do in Bunning.

"You ever read *Holes*?" Nero asks.

Ruby nods. "I loved it."

"I didn't read it for a long time. I thought it was going to be about a donut shop. Once I found out it was about something else, I was mad that I hadn't read it sooner."

"I know," Ruby says. "You get this idea of what something is like, and that gets in the way of finding out what it's *really* like."

"Exactly." Nero looks straight at Ruby. She gets this feeling he's not just talking about books and that he's going to ask some sort of crazy Nero DeNiro question, and suddenly Ruby understands how all her teachers must feel, torn between curiosity and the fear of losing control of things.

"Did you know that a donut is not a circle?" Ruby says quickly. "It's a torus. Like an inner tube."

"See? You might think you know all about Ruby

Pepperdine, but then she pops out this weird lit-tle fact and you think, how'd she know that? And why?"

Poke. Poke.

"It's just this thing I'm sort of interested in, maybe."

"*Maybe* you're interested in it?"

"Tori—that's the plural of torus—they're . . ." What were they? "They are unchanged by homeo-morphisms, such as bending or stretching."

"Homeomorphisms," Nero repeats.

"Such as bending or stretching," Ruby says. She waits for Nero to say something, to ask the right question so she'll know whether homeomorphism has anything to do with making her wish come true.

"Why are you interested in homeomorphisms?" he asks.

That is not the right question.

Ruby tries something else. "Have you ever thought about time travel?"

"Every day at seven a.m. I wish I could travel to

two thirty so I could go play Frisbee. Or come here."
He looks at Ruby in that Nero way again.

Poke.

"What about backwards? Did you ever want to travel back in time?"

"Sure," says Nero. "Lots of times. I'd go check out the real ancient wonders, for one thing. Have a chat with Callimachus."

"Anything else? Would you go back in your own past?"

"Do I have a time machine? Can I go back as often as I want? Or is this more like a wish thing? Can I only go back once?"

"Once," says Ruby. "Just for a minute or two, and then you're back to now."

"A minute or two?" Nero shakes his hair out of his eyes, and Ruby can see his forehead crinkle. "So really you're asking what I'd want to relive — like the very best minute of my life?"

Or the worst, Ruby thinks.

"Can I reserve the wish for when I'm older? Like maybe when I'm a geezer I'm going to want to

114

relive the moment I became the president of Pixar or I scored the winning goal at the World Cup or I met my first girlfriend, or, um, you know, something." Nero's face is suddenly red. "I should go," he says. "We've got a paper-goods delivery today. I need to help my mom."

You need to help me, Ruby thinks. "Will you be here tomorrow?" she asks instead.

Nero shoves his phone into his backpack. "Unless I get a time machine. Then, who knows?"

The library had taken longer than Ruby wanted, and she has to run back to the theater. She is still breathing hard when she drops into her seat.

"Gingerbread kids!" the director calls. A dozen eight- and nine-year-olds shuffle onto the stage to sing their "Not As Sweet As You Think We Are" song, and the rest of the cast wanders out into the auditorium. Ruby spies her "Be right back" note and has just enough time to hide it in her backpack before Lucy perches on the seat beside her.

"What did you think?" she whispers to Ruby,

and then, even more quietly, "What did *you* think? What did you *think*?" This thing she is doing with her play lines has spilled over into her non-Gretel lines too.

"It was good," Ruby says. "You were good."

"That's it? What about the oven scene?"

Oven scene? Rats.

"I had to go to the library for a little bit," Ruby admits. "I missed a few things."

"What?" Lucy says it loud enough to make one of the assistant directors turn around and stare at them.

"Mind like water," Ruby whispers.

"Fine," Lucy whispers back. "But you should have been here. I did this karate move when I knocked the witch into the oven." She demonstrates, giving a high sideways kick. "The director said it was cool, but maybe not the mood we were going for. Besides, it is kind of hard to kick in a dirndl." *Kick* in a dirndl. Kick in a *dirndl*. "Anyway, I wish you'd stick around. I feel like I do better when you're here."

"I'll be here for the rest of rehearsal," Ruby assures her, but Lucy is still grumpy.

"If you'd *seen* it, though. I mean, Gretel has guts and I thought . . ." Lucy continues.

If Ruby had a time machine, she'd go back and watch that part of the rehearsal. But if she did, would the time she spent watching the rehearsal become the real time? Would it mean that she would not have had her conversation with Nero? Or . . .

" . . . so do you think I should try it?"

"Huh? Try what?"

"Dang, Ruby," Lucy says. "Even when you're here you're not here."

The Karate Kid

◦ ◉ ◦

Ruby hears her before she sees her. The crack of the board, the *Kiai!* yell. Okeda Martial Arts is making its way around Cornelius Circle.

"*Hi-ya!*" says Willow, chopping Ruby in the stomach.

Aunt Rachel grabs hold of Willow's wrist. "We don't hit."

"I didn't hit. I chopped."

"We don't chop, either. Now check in with Ruby."

"Is your belly okay, Ruby?" Willow asks. Her concern is not very convincing.

"Yes," Ruby says, even though it is not. This is not Willow's fault, however. Ruby's belly was hurting even before her cousin chopped it.

"Kiai!"

Ruby hears the crack of another board. She can see Mr. Fisch's pickup truck now. It is black with OKEDA MARTIAL ARTS painted on the door. Just beyond, Ruby can see the glistening bald head of Mr. Fisch as he reaches into the truck bed for another thin square board. Behind him, about ten feet back, walk two rows of *gi*-clad students. One at a time, the students dart ahead of the rest and bow to Mr. Fisch, and then, with a few graceful steps, approach the board Mr. Fisch holds out. *"Kiai!"* A sharp kick and the board is split in half.

Lucy is the youngest of his students in the parade. She is also the fiercest. Ruby has never seen her look so fierce. In past parades Lucy has performed kicks and punches in the air but never attacked a board. This year things are different.

Lucy does not look at Ruby. She looks only at

the square of wood, even when it is not her turn. But now it is her turn. She steps forward, her eyes never leaving the board her dad holds.

"*Kiai!*" she cries. *Crack!*

Lucy bows, then turns and dashes back to her place in line.

If you were Ruby Pepperdine, you might think that was pretty impressive. You might think about calling out your friend Lucy's name and cheering and waving. You might hope that your friend would hear your voice and smile when she sees your face in the crowd.

Or you might wonder if Lucy has already seen your face. If she has been imagining it every time she approaches one of those boards. If she imagines your face and then *Kiai!*

You might decide it is better not to say anything at all.

To Tell or Not to Tell

◦ ◉ ◦

There are two schools of thought about the secrecy of wishes. One is that you should always tell, because you never know who might be able to help you get what you wished for. People who believe this often appear on talk shows. Share your dreams with the Universe, they say.

The other school holds the birthday candle philosophy: to tell a wish is to ruin its chances of happening.

Ever since she became Essay Girl, Ruby has thought of her wish as the birthday candle sort, but now, as she swirls her spoon in her morning Cheerios, she is beginning to reconsider her position. She is surprised to discover that talking to Nero about time travel has actually made her feel a little better, even though she isn't any closer to understanding what it is she is supposed to do. What if telling somebody the truth about her wish would help her figure it out?

What kind of wish is a Captain Bunning wish? she wonders. *Would telling—or not telling—ruin things?*

"No, Maurice, I will *not* be in the service center tomorrow," Ruby's dad says into his phone. "Tomorrow is Bunning Day, remember? The parade?"

Once again Ruby is careful not to wish for a sign of what she is supposed to do. But, she tells the Universe, if a sign just happened to come her way, she wouldn't mind a bit.

That is when her phone rings.

"Ruby?"

It is Lucy. Thank you, Universe! Clearly, she is supposed to tell her wish to Lucy.

"Can I come over early today?" Ruby says.

"*Exactly* what I was going to ask," says Lucy.

A sign for sure, Ruby thinks. But later, when Aunt Rachel drops her off at Okeda Martial Arts, Lucy drags Ruby into her dad's office, pushes her into a desk chair, and drops the *Hansel and Gretel* script into her lap.

"I am *so* glad you're here. I need to go through the second act," she says. She looks pajama-party tired, but she is talking quickly, like people do on game shows and 911 calls. "Hansel starts." Lucy points to a line at the top of the page. "Say, 'Oh, Gretel, I wish we were back home.'"

Clearly, the Universe thinks Ruby needs to wait a bit before engaging in wish talk. Fine, she can wait. A little while, anyway.

"Oh, Gretel. I wish we were back home."

Lucy bites her bottom lip. "What's my line?"

"'Do not fret' . . ." Ruby reads.

"Stop. I got it." Lucy puts on her Inner Gretel voice. "Do not fret, brother. I am *working* on a plan. Working on a *plan* . . . Which is better?"

Ruby is not sure, but it doesn't matter. Lucy has moved on. Inner Gretel is telling Hansel that he must keep his chin up, that he must trust her, that all will be well.

Of course all will be well, Ruby thinks. This is a play. There's a whole script here. As long as everyone says the right lines, the play will move on, page by page, scene by scene, straight through to the happy ending. Just like it is supposed to.

"Ruby. It's your turn."

"Sorry." Ruby turns a page and finds Hansel's next line. "No, sister. Run away. Save yourself."

"Shhh, Hansel — she's coming!" *She's* coming.

For more than an hour, Ruby sits at Mr. Fisch's desk, reading through the second act, being Hansel. Being the witch. Singing gingerbread songs.

"I feel better now," Lucy says, flopping onto the couch Mr. Fisch keeps for karate people who get kicked too hard and need to lie down for a minute. "I mean, I'm still forgetting some things, but I know I'm improving. Maybe you could take some notes at rehearsal and we can go over them afterward?" An alarm sounds on Lucy's phone. "Yikes!" she says, leaping from the couch. "We'd better hurry up! This director is a total stickler about being late."

Ruby swings her backpack over her shoulder and follows her friend out to the sidewalk. It is a five-minute walk to the theater. Plenty of time to explain about her wish and Gigi and everything. *Now,* Ruby thinks. *I will tell Lucy about my wish now.* But Lucy keeps talking.

"So when the witch is coming after me, do you think I ought to be more scared or more angry?" Lucy asks. "I think maybe I should start out all panicky and then . . ."

Ruby only half listens as she follows Lucy down the street, past the hardware store, past the stationery shop, past Delish, which is so full of customers that Ruby cannot see if Nero is inside.

". . . except every time Fiona cackles, she, like, totally covers up my lines, you know? Maybe we could practice that part while we're walking?"

At the corner they cut across Cornelius Circle to Memorial Park. Lucy flips through the script pages, looking for the "Chasing Gretel" scene. She finds it just as they reach the statue of Captain Bunning. He stands tall at the edge of the park, looking up through the hole in his famous donut. The sun gleams on his coat buttons.

This is it, Ruby thinks. *I'm going to tell her now.*

"I wanted to—" Ruby says, but she is interrupted by the buzz of her cell phone. DELISH it says on the screen. "Go on ahead. I'll catch up," she tells Lucy.

Lucy frowns. "I guess I can go over my songs. But hurry, okay?" She walks ahead, singing about searching for crumbs and losing one's way.

"Hello?"

"The Grand Canyon," says Nero.

"What?"

"I was seven. My whole family went on vacation to the Grand Canyon. If I could wish myself back to any time, it would be then. Not a donut for miles. Now what about you? What's your wish?"

Maybe *this* is the sign. Maybe she's supposed to tell *Nero* her wish. But how can she know for sure?

"You sound like a genie," says Ruby, stalling. She hopes he will go off on one of his question tangents, asking why genies were always stuck in bottles and lamps but never in cans or packing crates, but he does not.

"Is it embarrassing?"

"It's private."

"Oh."

"Wait. It's not that I don't want to tell you. It's just that . . ." Ruby thinks carefully. She does not want to mess this up. "My quarter went through Captain Bunning's donut," she says. "On my birthday."

"Whoa," says Nero. "Did you wish for something good?"

"Something important."

"A time travel thing?"

"Maybe. I don't know."

"How can you not know?"

"I wished . . . I wished that something had been different. In the past."

"Which is why you care about homeomorphism," said Nero.

"What?"

"I have mad Google skills, Ruby Tuesday. I read about tori and homeomorphism and time and all that," Nero says.

There is a connection between donuts and time? Maybe this is the sign. "What did you learn?" Ruby says.

"I have mad *Google* skills, Ruby. Not mad physics skills. I didn't really get it. But you get it, right?"

"No," she says. "I didn't even know about the time thing. I just want to—" She stops herself. "I just want my wish to come true."

"Your quarter went through the donut, right? I'd say you're good."

"But I'm not good." How is she supposed to explain this? "I don't feel good. You know how when you're solving a story problem in math and you have an answer but it doesn't feel quite done yet? Like you're missing something? I have a missing-something feeling."

"You sure it's because of your wish?" says Nero. "What if you're missing something else?"

She is missing something else. Someone else. But so is her dad, and her mom, and all the rest of the Pepperdine family, and they're just fine. No, it has to be about her wish. And once she figures everything out, she'll feel fine too. "I'm not missing anything else," Ruby says. "Except whatever was on that website."

"Meet me at the library. If you want. You don't have to tell me what you wished for or anything, but, you know, we could look at the site together. I could help."

It would be good to have Nero's help. "Two heads are better than one," Ruby says.

"Not always," says Nero. "Like if you were at the store trying to buy a shirt, it would be hard to fit two heads through a regular neck hole. Or if—"

Ruby's phone buzzes. It's a text from Lucy.

Where r u?!!!

By the time Ruby gets to the theater, Lucy is already onstage.

"How could we have forgotten . . ." Inner Gretel stops. "Ugh. What's the line?"

"'How could we have forgotten about those pesky birds,'" says the director.

"Right. Okay. Those pesky birds. Those *pesky* birds," Lucy says. "Those pesky *birds*."

Ruby sits in the second row from the back, where she always does. She looks toward the stage, but she doesn't see it. Not really. She is thinking. About wishes and signs and homeomorphisms. She finds a scrap paper in her backpack and writes a note.

Dropping off book at library.
Back in a flash! Promise!

Wanting a Circle

◉ ◉ ◉

The kids from the Playground Day Camp are Hula-Hooping down Cornelius Circle. Twelve kids, sixteen hoops. Some are rolling them. Some whirl them around their middles or on their arms. One girl, Serendipity Olmstead, spins a hoop around one ankle, skipping over it with every step. She has been doing this since the beginning of the parade, and even though her legs are super tired, she will continue to kick and skip all the way around Cornelius Circle and up Main Street and into the rec center parking lot, because she has a bet with her brother Chance that she can, and when she succeeds, Chance will have to call Serendipity "Your Majesty" for a whole week.

"I want a circle!" Carter-Ann yells.

"It's a Hula-Hoop," says Willow.

"We have one at home in the garage," Aunt Rachel says. "Maybe Ruby will get it out for you at the cookout. I hope I have enough ribs."

Every year after the Bunning Day Parade is over, the entire family—Mom's side and Dad's—gathers in Aunt Rachel's backyard, where Uncle Jay has spent the whole day preparing a cookout feast. Everyone eats and talks about who was in what car and what the mayor said to the Bunning Day Queen and whether any of the city council members spoke to any of the other city council members until, for a little while, everyone stops talking and chews. And then they talk some more, and then Gigi brings out ice cream and a huge pan of her famous apple crisp.

Ruby wonders if Uncle Jay will be making the apple crisp this year. She doubts it. Gigi didn't leave behind a recipe. It was one of those things, like how to fix a Fiat or where to find the Seven Sisters constellation in the night sky, that Gigi knew by heart.

Ruby sorts through her note cards again. She should have learned her speech by heart. Maybe she was supposed to have. Maybe she was supposed to say her speech exactly right—not a stumble, not a mistake. What if she messed it up? Would her wish get messed up too?

> Then he came here. It was just a big field and some woods and not many people, but he was tired of drifting around. He

Across the street the red-haired family bob their heads in time with Serendipity's Hula-Hoop, much the way people who are watching Olympic ski jumpers lean forward or bowlers curve their bodies as their ball arcs toward the pins. *Why do people do this when they know it won't change what happens?* Ruby wonders.

This is not the sort of thing Ruby used to

wonder. But this wish has her thinking about things like that. This wish, and being around Nero.

Once, Ruby remembers, Nero even questioned Mr. Cipielewski about a circle being 360 degrees.

Mr. Cipielewski taught them about degrees in math. A triangle has 90 degrees. A circle has 360.

"What," Nero had said, "if you only have 359 degrees?"

"Then you do not have a circle," said Mr. Cipielewski.

"What do you have?"

"Nothing," said Mr. Cipielewski. "Nothing we have a name for, Nero. Nothing we're going to learn about in sixth grade."

But it couldn't be nothing, could it? All that effort of going around and around and just missing things by one degree? Then it would be *nothing*?

Ruby peeks over the bobbing red heads and at the Delish tent, just as she has seventeen times before, every time there is a break between parade entries or someone walks by with a bag of donuts. Sometimes she sees Nero looking at the parade and sometimes he is looking at his dad and one time he was looking straight up at the ceiling of the Delish tent. But always, every time, he is not looking at Ruby.

Which is her own fault.

A week ago he had been just another boy in her class. Then a few days later they were friends. Or about to be friends. Like 359 degrees of a friendship. But that was before Ruby said what she said.

Was it possible that now they really were nothing?

The Hole That Turns
Things Inside Out

◉ ◉ ◉

When Ruby enters the children's room at the library, she finds Nero at one of the computer carrels. "Look at this," he says, pointing to the wiki page on the screen in front of him. Right in the center of the page is an illustration of a torus. It looks like a blue donut with a small black spot on its side.

"It has a hole poked in it," Ruby says.

"I know. Sit down." The other computer carrels are full and the rest of the chairs have elves and Orclords in them. Nero scootches over. He is skinny enough that they can share a seat, though his shoulders bump against hers and threaten to knock her off the chair.

Nero clicks on ANIMATE, and the illustration on the screen changes. The small black hole opens wide and stretches back over the rest of the torus, like it is swallowing it. The lining of the torus — which is orange in this picture — flips out and the blue side disappears. "The outside becomes the inside, and the inside becomes the outside," Nero says.

Ruby watches as the hole stretches and the torus turns inside out again. It's kind of cool, except that . . . "No matter which side it's on, it's always got that hole poked in it."

Nero takes his eyes off the computer and looks at Ruby through his bangs. "There'd be no way for it to go inside out otherwise. The hole is what lets it change."

Poke. Poke.

They are sitting very close together, and Nero's eyes look bigger than usual. "Is that the time travel part?" Ruby asks quickly.

"It's related. I think." Nero scrolls to another animation. This time the torus is white. The left side swells and stretches while the right side gets skinnier, until one side looks as fat as a coffee cup and the other as thin as its handle. "That's homeomorphism. The shape can stretch, but it keeps certain properties — it's still a tube-y, torus kind of thing."

Ruby watches as the shape slowly returns to its original donut form. "What does it have to do with time travel?"

"Okay, so, how I read it is this: Einstein said that time is relative, right?"

Ruby has heard that before — on a coffee commercial. "Right."

"And time moves in a line, right?"

Ruby has seen timelines. There is a timeline mural in the lobby of city hall.

"And tori — they're like lots of lines in a donut shape, right?"

Like the webbing illustration. Like Spider-Man Donut. "Right."

"Okay, so, what this says is the space inside a torus can stretch in one place and shrink in another, and that shifts the relationship of the lines to one another. Some get closer and some get farther away. And space and time work together and change together, and, um, after that I don't really get it."

Ruby reads the words on the computer screen. She doesn't really get it either.

But at the end of the page there is a quote from Albert Einstein. "When a man sits with a pretty girl for an hour, it seems like a minute. But let him sit on a hot stove for a minute and it's longer than any hour. That's relativity."

That she gets.

Her last minutes with Gigi sped by so fast, they were hardly minutes. But since Gigi died, since Ruby made her wish, they have stretched so much that it feels like they are still happening. In her thoughts. In her dreams. In the poke, poke, poke of right now.

"It's all coming together," Gigi had gasped. Ruby hears it like it is happening again right now, like she is in her living room standing in front of the recliner. "Listen," Gigi says. And Ruby hears her, exactly as if she had stepped back in time.

This is why Ruby does not notice the door to the children's room swing open.

It is why she does not see Lucy come in.

It is why she is startled out of her seat when Lucy says "Aha!" in an Inner Stepsister voice. "This is where you sneak off to!"

Ruby gets to her feet. Her voice is wobbly. "Didn't you see my note?"

"Your note said you were coming here to return your books. It didn't say you were coming to meet your boyfriend."

"He's not my boyfriend." He is *not* her boyfriend. He isn't. They hardly even know each other. "We hardly even know each other."

"But instead of helping me like you promised, you come here to be with him."

Ruby feels a rush of heat on her face.

"We're working on her wish," Nero says. Ruby's hand claps to her mouth, even though she did not say a word.

"Her *wish*? What are you talking about?"

Ruby does not look at Nero, but out of the corner of her eye she can see that he is looking at her.

"You're supposed to be my best friend," Lucy snaps.

"I am." She cannot lose her best friend. She cannot. She and Lucy have always been friends. Rucy and Luby. She can't lose Gigi and Lucy. Not both.

"But you told your *boyfriend* about some important *wish* and you didn't tell me?"

"He's not my boyfriend," Ruby sputters. "We're not even friends. He's just here at the library at the same time I am."

Over at the round tables, an elf shouts with glee. "You are dead, Panoptocles! You are an ex-druid."

"There's no wish," Nero says. "I made it up. I'm weird like that."

Lucy's eyes burn on Ruby's, then she turns and stomps away.

Without a word Ruby follows, hurrying down

the stairs and out of the library. "Wait!" she calls. She finally catches up to Lucy on the lawn.

"What wish?" says Lucy.

"I made a wish. On my birthday. It's about Gigi."

"Go on."

"I can't tell you," Ruby says. "It might—"

"But you can tell *him?*"

"I didn't—" Ruby starts to say, but Lucy cannot hear her.

"He didn't even know Gigi!" Lucy yells. "*I* did. We're *supposed* to be best friends! I tell you *everything* and you didn't tell *me* anything!"

Ruby searches for something to say, something that has calmed Lucy down before. "Mind like water," she says.

"This is not a stupid pebble, Ruby Pepperdine! This is a meteor! You have hurled an enormous *meteor* into the lake of our friendship. You've caused a tsunami!"

Lucy runs off, but Ruby does not know if she

should follow. She has no idea what she is supposed to do. Where she is supposed to go.

She turns and looks back at the library, up to the second-floor window where the children's room is — just in time to see Nero turn his back and walk away.

One More Time

⊙ ◉ ⊙

Ruby shuffles through her index cards one more time.

She reads her essay one more time, although when the sixth and seventh cards stick together, she doesn't notice.

Maybe it is supposed to be this way. Maybe in order to get her wish she has to be friendless. It doesn't seem particularly fair, but maybe Captain Bunning isn't about fair. She didn't say he was fair in her essay. She said he was famous. She said he built a school. She said he started the town.

from the woods, he salvaged beams from
his beloved *Evangeline* and built a school.
    Then he went traveling again —this

The redheaded family must be getting un-
comfortable on their milk crates, because most of
them have stood up. Ruby cannot see the Delish
tent now.

When her wish comes true, it will be worth it. It
has to be worth it.

Things will be back how they were supposed
to be.

Ruby will have listened and Gigi will have explained. Or something. And then Ruby wouldn't
have needed to make a wish at all. And Lucy
would be her friend. And Nero—well, probably she wouldn't have gotten to know Nero. Or
be Essay Girl, either. And maybe there are some
other things that might be bad about it. Or different—

If only she had a sign to tell her things were

going to work out. Not a formula or a question or a webbed-over donut. A sign. A clear, simple, un-mix-up-able sign.

Mr. Victor Gomez

⊙ ◉ ⊙

Most of the year Mr. Victor Gomez is accounts manager at New Hampshire Bank and Trust. He wears a dress shirt and tie, flat-fronted pants and cordovan shoes. His desk is tidy. Shipshape, people might say, in part because next to his desk lamp is a bottle with a ship in it. *Evangeline.* Mr. Gomez loves *Evangeline.* He also loves Captain Bunning.

This is why, on Bunning Day, Mr. Gomez does not wear his dress shirt and tie, his flat-fronted pants and cordovan shoes. Instead, Mr. Gomez puts on black boots and saggy wool pants and a dark wool coat with brass buttons. He pulls a wool cap down tight on his head and slips a pipe between his teeth.

When he looks in the mirror, he does not see Mr. Gomez, accounts manager. He sees Captain Cornelius Bunning. He can almost smell the sea.

Perhaps this is why, while all the other members of the Bunning Historical Society's parade contingent are sweating in their almost historically accurate period costumes, Mr. Gomez looks cool as, well, an ocean breeze.

All around him, ladies dressed as Leticia Bunning carry pails filled with donut-shaped coupons that will grant the bearer free admission to the Bunning Historical Society Museum.

All around Ruby, kids wave their arms frantically, calling, "Me!" and "I didn't get one!" This despite the fact that every year, every school-aged one of them will visit that museum at least once on a field trip. Later, when the parade is over, this coupon, along with the bumper stickers for state senate candidates and some kale-flavored candies from the food co-op, will be left on the floor of their parents' car.

Mr. Gomez does not mind the frantic children.

He sees the parade through different eyes, imagining it, as he always does, a welcome parade for Captain Bunning—a cheering crowd in awe of his mastery of *Evangeline* in the face of a freak storm. Through Mr. Gomez's eyes, it is possible to see this crowd without its soda cans and helium balloons. It is possible to see them in jerkins and laborer's cloth, some of them still holding the tools of their trade. With Bunning-like majesty, Mr. Gomez waves at them. The farmer and his wife. The miller and his redheaded family.

And over there, that brown-haired girl of eleven or twelve, clutching a stack of blue cards. She meets his eyes with such hope and admiration. Mr. Gomez gives her a reassuring smile. He feels compelled to nod at her. "Yes," he says before he turns his eyes elsewhere. *Good common people,* he thinks. *They have erected a statue in my honor.*

He raises his arm like the statue, holding aloft a donut that only he can see.

Captain Bunning Said Yes

◉ ◉ ◉

Ruby had not imagined it. She had been standing in the circle in the square, holding her note cards to her chest, wondering if maybe she had gotten things mixed up. If she was seeing signs where there weren't any. What if she had lost her best friend over nothing? What if time didn't stretch? What if there were no spokes? What if? . . .

Her thoughts had been interrupted by Willow's squeals. "It's the fish and chips man! The man on the Salty Sea Dog Fish and Chips box!" She was pointing to a man in a dark wool coat and cap walking stiffly among the other volunteers from the Bunning Historical Society.

"That's not a fish and chips man," Ruby had said. "That's Captain Bunning. Didn't you go to the museum last year?"

"I missed it. I had the flu." Willow waved her arm desperately for whatever it was those long-skirted ladies were handing out.

Ruby had kept her eye on Captain Bunning.

And then Captain Bunning seemed to look right at her. He smiled.

Ruby did not wish that he would tell her that she was doing what she was supposed to do, but she asked the question hard in her head.

"Yes," he said. He said yes.

"Ruby, look!" Willow waved the paper a volunteer had given her. "Look, Ruby! I get a free donut! That says 'free' right there."

Ruby read the old-fashioned writing that curled around the circumference of the coupon. "It says you get 'Free Admission to the Glorious Past.'"

Willow scrunched up her face. "I'd rather have a donut."

Ruby looked again at Captain Bunning, who

was now walking away from her. He had said yes. Her wish was about to come true, wasn't it?

Captain Bunning raised his arm then, just like his statue in Cornelius Circle, and Ruby could come to no other conclusion.

It was.

The Schoolhouse
Approaches

◉ ◉ ◉

"There it is! Look, Carter-Ann! There's the school!"

Carter-Ann peers down the road to where her mother is pointing, but she does not see the school. She knows what it looks like, because Willow is in kindergarten there. The school is almost as big as the grocery store, but it doesn't have food, and the floors have squares on them and she can hop from one blue square to another all the way to the drinking fountain, which is too tall up and gets water all over her chin and her shirt, but she can't help it because as soon as she sees it, she gets thirsty.

"I'm thirsty," she says.

Her mother hands her a water bottle, but it is empty. "I already drunked it. I want juice."

"It will have to wait," her mother says. "Ruby is going to do her thing in a minute. As soon as the school gets here."

Carter-Ann looks again. She still does not see Willow's school. And, anyway, schools don't move. They stay put, like houses and car dealerships and grocery stores. That is why you have to put your seat belt on and drive everyplace.

"I'm thirsty," she says again.

"Carter-Ann, just—just, you'll have to wait."

She always has to wait. That's her whole life. People telling her to wait. Or to hurry up. The only time anybody hurries up for her is when she has to go to the bathroom.

"I have to go to the bathroom," she says. And it's true. She didn't have to a second ago, but now that she has said it out loud, she has to. Bad.

"Now? Oh, Carter-Ann, can it wait just one minute?"

Sometimes if Carter-Ann has to pee really bad,

she crosses her legs and it is better, so she crosses her legs, but it is not better. "I have to go now," she says. She makes the word *now* really long, so her mom will understand. *Noooooooooooow.*

"Ruby?" her mother says. She has to say it twice, because Cousin Ruby is thinking about something. "Ruby? I'm sorry. Carter-Ann has to go to the bathroom."

"It's okay," Cousin Ruby says. Cousin Ruby is always good and never gets in trouble. At restaurants she can go to the bathroom by herself. Nobody has to go with her.

"Willow? Willow, honey, you're going to have to come with me," Mom says.

Willow looks mad. "I'm going to miss some candy."

Carter-Ann had not thought about missing some candy. "I don't have to go," she says, but her legs are almost double-crossed now.

"We're going," Mom says. "Wish Ruby good luck."

Ruby doesn't need good luck. She already has

good luck. She is big and can stay behind where the candies are. But Willow says good luck and Carter-Ann doesn't want to look like a baby. "Wish," she says, and then her mom is tugging her away from the parade, telling her, like always, to hurry up.

What Did You Think
Would Happen?

◎ ◉ ◎

If you were Bunning Day Essay Girl or Boy, you
would likely have rehearsed this moment in your
head many times. You would have imagined Bunning Elementary School librarian Ms. Kemp-Davie
hopping out of the pickup truck and hurrying to
the back of the trailer on which the model schoolhouse was secured. You would have seen her place
the step stool next to the trailer, seen her climb up
onto it, seen her reach in the schoolhouse window
to grab the microphone and flip on the amplification system. And you would have seen yourself
there too, stepping one-two-three up the step stool
(if you were Effie Stefanopolis, Essay Girl in 2007,

you would have even practiced going up and down a ladder at home a few times) and listening as Ms. Kemp-Davie said what she always did. That for her, the highlight of every Bunning Day was this moment, when the winner of the Bunning Day Essay Contest joined her here in front of this symbol of education to which Captain Bunning was so dearly dedicated. Here, to read her winning essay, was — and you would have imagined hearing Ms. Kemp-Davie say your name.

Which is why Ruby is surprised when the pickup truck door opens and it is not Ms. Kemp-Davie who exits but a tall, thin man with wide glasses and a beard.

Suddenly, Patsy Whelk is at Ruby's side. "Okay, kid. Your turn."

It is her turn.

Up on the trailer, the thin man has switched on the mike.

"Hello," he says into it.

Most of the kids in the crowd say hello back.

"I'm, um, the new middle school librarian, Paul

Yellich, and this is my first Bunning Day, and, um, it's really great." Paul Yellich squints at a note card in his hand and realizes he is wearing the wrong glasses. He needs his reading glasses. The words on his card are squiggles. "So, you all know what comes next. The essay contest winner . . ." He is supposed to say something else, but he cannot remember it. He does, however, remember the girl's name. "I'm very proud to introduce Ruthie Pepper, who is going to come on up here and do what you've all been waiting for."

This is not going right, thinks Mr. Yellich.

Nothing is going right, thinks Ruby as she steps up onto the trailer.

How can her wish be about to come true when Ms. Kemp-Davie isn't here? When this man can't even get her name right?

"Ruthie Pepper, everybody!" The man holds the microphone out, and Ruby takes it.

"Thank you," she says, even though she would rather say her name is not Ruthie, it is Ruby. Thank you is what she says. Just like she is supposed to.

Ruby looks down at her note cards. At the chocolate swirl that is Willow's fingerprint. *Some say it was destiny.*

That, of course, is what Ms. Kemp-Davie would have expected to hear. But Ms. Kemp-Davie is, at this very moment, in Greece, viewing one of Callimachus's favorite hangouts.

The only other people who have any idea what is written on those cards are not near enough to hear Ruby either. Her mom and dad are just now pulling into the rec center parking lot. Aunt Rachel is holding the door of a porta-potty closed for Carter-Ann.

Nobody knows what Ruby is supposed to say.

And for a moment, Ruby is not sure either.

"Listen," Gigi had told her.

That's it! That is what she is supposed to do!

"I'm listening," Ruby says.

What Ruby Does

⊙ ◉ ⊙

Twenty seconds can be quick if you are on the phone with a friend or spinning around on the Christmas Carousel at Santa's Village or holding the hand of someone you love.

But if you are holding your breath, twenty seconds can be a long time.

And if you are standing on the sidewalk of a parade route and the girl on the float in front of you is not doing anything, twenty seconds can be a really, really long time.

And if you are a brand-new librarian and you feel responsible for the fact that this girl on the float—this Ruthie—is holding a microphone and not speaking at all, twenty seconds can feel like your whole entire life.

Which is why, in your kindest voice, you might say her name. "Ruthie?"

And you might even be relieved to hear her speak into the microphone. "I have a minute," you might hear her say. "I'd like it to be a minute of silence. For my grandmother Genevieve Pepperdine, who loved this parade and this town so much."

Not Pepper. Pepper*dine*, you might think. In fact, that is all you might think for the next forty seconds. Pepper*dine*. Pepper*dine*. And how you looked like such an idiot and what a brilliant way to start off in a new town, messing up the name of the essay kid, and how you wish you could open up the door to the model schoolhouse and hide inside.

Which is why you would not notice that in front of you, the essay kid is leaning forward, stretching forward, looking like she is straining to hear through the silence.

* * *

"I'm listening," Ruby had said out loud. And in her head she says it again. *I'm listening. I'm listening, Gigi. I am sorry, I am so sorry I didn't listen before. I was scared. Maybe. I didn't know.*

You weren't supposed to die, Gigi. Everybody said it. You weren't that old. And you had such life. I didn't know what to do. I did what I thought I was supposed to do.

Poke, poke, poke. Ruby feels the poking in her chest.

The pricking in her eyes.

Is it Gigi? Is it Gigi zipping back along whatever radius line she has found, coming to make things okay again?

Silence.

That is what Ruby needs. She has been talking—even if it was only in her head—when all this time she was supposed to be listening! Isn't that what Gigi said? "Listen"?

All around, Ruby hears the sounds of the town. The grownups—at least the ones who had heard and were paying attention—are quiet. A few of the kids are too, and one boy salutes like he did at the funeral of his uncle who died in Afghanistan. But some people are chatting and some are scolding their children. Some are singing along with the banjo band that can still be heard from the far side of Cornelius Circle.

Shut up! Ruby tells them in her head. She tries to push the banjo sounds away, but they grow louder. *Shut up! I am listening for Gigi. Or time or things getting fixed or whatever it is I'm supposed to hear. Whatever Gigi wanted me to know.*

Boom! A Civil War cannon goes off somewhere down the route and babies bawl. Ruby tries to push those sounds away too, but more noise fills in. The motor of the pickup truck, the horn of a Shriner car, the *ting-ting-ting* of something metal tapping against the bronze shoe of the Bunning statue. A distant *crack*—maybe Lucy splitting boards with Okeda Martial Arts. And—is it possible?—the sizzle of donuts at the Delish tent, where Nero is.

Every small impossible sound crowds in the way of what she is supposed to hear.

No! Ruby thinks. *Be quiet! I'm supposed to be listening. I need to listen. I need—*

Ruby feels Mr. Yellich's hand on her shoulder.

"Time's up, Ruthie."

The End

◎ ◉ ◎

Aunt Rachel is not near the circle in the square when Ruby returns to it. Neither is Willow or Carter-Ann or Baby Amelia. Ruby has been on the schoolhouse float for only a minute and a half. It takes longer than a minute and a half to find a bathroom on Bunning Day.

The parade continues on its path.

Nothing has changed.

Whatever it was that she was supposed to have done is still undone. Whatever was supposed to have happened to make things okay didn't happen. None of the things that Ruby imagined—seeing

Gigi's smiling face or hearing whatever it was that Gigi had wanted to say or traveling back in time (which, okay, she didn't really think would happen, except maybe, but not *really* really) — none of it happened.

What happened was that Ruby had stood on the steps of the schoolhouse float and didn't even read her stupid essay. Which was probably what she was really supposed to have done. And now she couldn't. Not ever. Things were never going to be like they were supposed to.

"Ruby! Ruby!" Carter-Ann has broken away from her mother. She is pulling at Ruby's wrist. "I almost fell in!"

"The porta-potty was an adventure," Aunt Rachel tells Ruby.

"Did we miss any candy?" asks Willow, pushing her way past Ruby to reclaim her spot at the curb. A clown from the hospital tosses a shower of SweeTarts, which sends Carter-Ann and Willow diving.

"Out of the street! Out of the street!" Aunt Rachel says. "How did it go? Ouch! Amelia, we don't bite!"

HOONK! HOOONNNK!

Red lights flash and Baby Amelia bursts into tears.

"It's the fire trucks!" shouts Carter-Ann.

"That means it's the end," says Willow. "Isn't it, Ruby?"

Ruby nods. It is the end.

What Makes You Safe

⊙ ◉ ⊙

Willow and Carter-Ann shoot invisible Spider-Man Donut webs all the way home. "Gotcha, Ruby!" they say. "You're stuck."

Eventually, Aunt Rachel's driveway fills with cars, and parents and aunts and uncles and cousins fill the picnic table and lawn chairs and shaded spots on the backyard grass. They heap paper plates with burgers and hot dogs and ribs—except for Cousin Fiona, who decided this afternoon after seeing the baby cows in the Fairmont Farms part of the parade that she will become a vegetarian. Her plate is heaped with fruit salad and macaroni salad and garden salad. She is pretending she does not know that the brown bits in the garden salad are bacon. There is no apple crisp.

Every plate is full and everyone is eating, except for Willow and Carter-Ann and a half dozen of Ruby's younger cousins, who are chasing one another around the yard, catching each other in invisible webs.

"Ruby is safe!" yells Willow as she dashes, panting, up to Ruby's chair. "You can't web me now."

"I can too," says Cousin Louie.

"Nuh-uh. That's the rule," Willow says. "Ruby is safe. Aren't you?"

"Are you safe?" Louie looks skeptical.

Willow's face is pink and her hair is curled with sweat. Her eyes plead.

"Of course," says Ruby.

"Okay. Ruby is safe," concedes Louie. "But you can only stay at safe for sixty seconds, and then you have to run again. That's the rule too."

Willow nods. "Thanks, Ruby."

Ruby pushes a tomato slice around her paper plate.

She thinks about rules.

About supposed to.

About not supposed to.

And about a third possibility. One she has been trying not to think about ever since Gigi died. One that makes her feel as small and lost as she does in her dream. As she did the first time Gigi told her about the swirling centerless space. But now there is no Gigi to find her in it.

What if there is no such thing as supposed to?

Getting There

◦ ◉ ◦

Every year, after the cookout, Ruby's family heads for The Hole Shebang. Every year they pack blankets and folding chairs and a cooler of soda and a thermos of hot cocoa for Aunt Lynn, who gets chilly sitting on the ground. Every year Ruby's dad says, "Let's take the scenic route." And then, every year, they avoid the traffic of downtown Bunning and drive the quieter roads along the edge of town, Ruby's parents in the front seat, Gigi and Ruby buckled up in back, singing Sweet Adelines tunes.

Except this year, of course.

This year Ruby is buckled in her seat, but there is no singing. Ruby leans her head against the window. What if there is no supposed to? What if there is no one way things are meant to be? What if it is all just random and spinny and wild?

They drive past her old school. Past her new school. Past New Hampshire Bank and Trust. Past the cemetery.

Her parents have the radio on WNHB. "The first literary description of something that might be considered donut-like appears in the work of the Ancient Greeks," explains a pinched-sounding woman.

"That's enough of that." Ruby's mother turns off the radio. "I heard what you did in the parade," she says to Ruby. "The silence? For Gigi? That was a nice gesture, sweetie."

"But nobody got to hear your essay," says Ruby's dad.

"That's okay."

Ruby sees her parents glance at each other. "Do you have it with you?" her dad asks. "You could read it to us."

Her essay cards are folded into her shorts

pocket, but Ruby does not feel like reading them. "I'll get carsick," she says. It is one of her parents' greatest fears that someone will throw up in a Pepperdine Motors vehicle.

"I'll read it, then." Mom sticks her hand over the seat, palm open, and Ruby drops her cards into it.

Ruby's mother clears her throat. "'Some say it was destiny,'" she reads, sounding a little like the pinched woman from the radio. "'A brave sea captain, a freak storm, and a platter of puffy dough balls.'"

Dad chuckles. "Puffy dough balls."

"'Donut holes made him famous, but being a sailor' . . . 'just a big field' . . . Um? Ruby? I think your cards are out of order?" Mom hands the cards back for Ruby to sort out. "Just read it, honey. You won't get sick. —How long does it take to read — a minute, right? That's not very long."

Ruby shuffles the cards around to their proper places.

"Go on," says Ruby's dad. "We're listening."

"'Some say it was destiny,'" Ruby reads.

* * *

Some say it was destiny. A brave sea captain, a freak storm, and a platter of puffy dough balls.

Donut holes made him famous, but being a sailor was what Captain Bunning loved. When he and his ship grew too old to sail, he didn't know what to do. He dry-docked *Evangeline* and moved from city to city, looking for a place to settle. He thought he'd never find a home on land.

Then he came here. It was just a big field and some woods and not many people, but he was tired of drifting around. He decided to stay. Rather than use trees from the woods, he salvaged beams from his beloved *Evangeline* and built a school.

Then he went traveling again — this time telling everyone he met about the school, the place, and what it would become. People listened and people came and a real town grew.

Maybe it was destiny. Maybe not.

All I know is that Captain Bunning didn't just invent the donut hole, he created a "hole" community.

And I'm glad he did.

There is a sniffle from the front seat. "Mom? You okay?"

"I'm fine," says Mom. "Your dad's the crybaby." It would have sounded like an insult if she hadn't said it so gently.

"Aw, Ruby, you remind me of my mother." Dad makes a teary smile at her in the rearview mirror. "It's like having a little bit of Gigi there in the back seat."

It is so weird to see her dad cry. He did on the day Gigi died and at the funeral, but since then he has seemed like exactly the same dad he was before. Busier at work, maybe, but otherwise the same.

"I miss her a lot, Dad," Ruby says.

"You do, Rubes?" He sounds genuinely surprised. "I thought I was the only one. My brothers and sisters, everybody seems normal and busy—but, yeah. I miss her every day. She left a hole..." Dad's voice skips in the middle of the word, and Ruby's mom rests a soft hand on his shoulder. "I'm okay, Ruby. Don't worry," he says.

"I'm not worried." In fact, Ruby feels better than she has in a while.

The turn signal clicks on, and Ruby's dad pulls into the rec center parking lot. He rolls down his window and waves to a Boy Scout with an orange flag. "Where do you want us?" he asks. His voice has returned to normal; Mom's hand has left his shoulder. It is like the past three minutes never happened. But Ruby knows they did.

The Boy Scout waves their car toward another Scout, who waves them toward another, who, by luck or fate or chance or whatever, is standing just two spots away from where Lucy is helping her dads take lawn chairs out of the back of the Okeda Martial Arts pickup truck.

Ruby's dad shuts off the car and unlocks the

doors. "Hey, Rubes," he says. "Maybe later this week we can go to the cemetery together? I'm sure I can sneak away from the show room for a bit."

"Okay," Ruby says. She knows saying yes and going to the cemetery will make her dad feel better, but — "Dad? How about we go to the roof, too? Of the dealership?"

"Oh, Ruby. I don't know anything about stars," he says.

"That's okay," says Ruby. "I'll teach you."

Ruby's mom tilts her head in the direction of the Okeda Martial Arts truck. "Did you see Lucy?"

The few times they have argued in the past, Ruby waited for Lucy to calm down and come to her. That's how Ruby knew it was safe to apologize. Then everything would continue exactly as it had before, Luby and Rucy, exactly how it was supposed to be. If she went to Lucy now, who knew what would happen?

"I see her, Mom," Ruby says.

She unbuckles.

The Hole Shebang

○ ◉ ○

At first it is awkward.

"Hi," says Ruby. Or maybe it is Lucy. It doesn't matter. One says hi and then the other does. "I—" they both say, and then each waits for the other to finish.

"Lucy," Mr. Okeda says, "we're going to claim a spot. Are you sitting with the Pepperdines again this year?"

Ruby looks at Lucy. Lucy looks at Ruby. "Yes," they say.

"Make sure you're with them before it gets dark," says Mr. Fisch. Lucy's dads head for the rec center soccer field. Ruby and Lucy head in the opposite direction.

There are two playgrounds at the Bunning Recreation Center. One has relatively new equipment that is molded plastic and has no sharp edges or rusty bolts or things you can get your fingers stuck in. That playground is mobbed with little kids and hovering parents. A bit farther back, however, is another playground—smaller and much older, built at a time before parents discovered all the ways a kid could get a concussion. There are no little kids here. No hovering parents. There is a swing set with chains hanging from it but no swings. There is a metal slide, the kind that can burn your legs on a sunny day, and a steel carousel that you can run and push and hop onto and spin.

This is where Ruby and Lucy are headed.

"I should have known you wouldn't be mad at me," Lucy says, "but I was kind of a jerk." She keeps talking as they reach the back playground. Reciting, really, as if this is a part she has rehearsed. "I was so stressed out with the play, and I keep messing up all my lines, and I overreacted. Usually, you help with the lines more and I guess I was kind of mad that you kept cutting out on me."

Ruby sits cross-legged on the carousel, but Lucy cannot sit still. She grabs hold of one of the carousel bars and pushes. "And it's a really big part, you know? And everything depends on me and—"

If you were Ruby Pepperdine, you would be listening to your friend Lucy, but you might be stuck thinking about that third possibility, too. Wondering how, if it were true, a person could find her place in the world. How things wouldn't just be wild and spinny and out of control all the time. You might wonder how anyone was really supposed to figure anything out.

And so, when Lucy says, ". . . and then I find you talking about some secret wish with Nero? You're *supposed* to be my best friend"—you might not be able to stop yourself from saying what you've been thinking all afternoon.

"What if there is no supposed to?"

Which might make Lucy stop talking.

"What?" she might say a moment later. "Of course there is a supposed to. Otherwise people would be, like, stealing and driving a hundred miles an hour and stuff."

"Those are laws," Ruby says. "Rules. It's different than friends. Different than most things." The carousel has stopped now, but Ruby feels like it is still turning underneath her. "I'm not *supposed* to be your best friend. I *am* your best friend. I choose to be your friend. Because I like you. Because you like me." The last part comes out more like a question than a statement.

"Of course I like you! Geez, Ruby." Lucy sits next to Ruby on the carousel edge. They can see the part of the parking lot where the parade floats are on display. People wander in and out and around the floats. A red-faced man in a Civil War costume holds a toddler on his shoulders. A cluster of girls pose for a photo in front of a cardboard dairy barn. "Smile, Your Majesty," they can hear the photographer call.

"No supposed to, huh?" Lucy says, finally.

Ruby shrugs. "I don't think so."

"I think you've been hanging around Nero too much." Lucy laughs, and Ruby does too, a little.

"Nero is my friend too, you know."

"I know," Lucy says. I *know*.

"At least, I hope he is." Ruby cannot help but remember how he'd turned away from the library window. How he hadn't looked at her as she stood in the circle in the square. Maybe he is not her friend.

There is only one way to find out. Ruby pulls her phone from her pocket. It has been turned off since Patsy Whelk told her to during the parade.

There is one message. It is from Nero.

Well?

Ruby texts back. **You at rec center?**

Yes

Meet us at old playground.

Us?

Me and Lucy

No thanks

Lucy has been reading over Ruby's shoulder. "I can go sit with my dads," she says.

"Stay," Ruby says to Lucy. **Come**, she texts Nero.

Three minutes can be a short time when you are sitting with a back-again friend. It can be a long time when you are waiting to find out if you have another.

Ruby watches the parking lot. One after another, people emerge from cars and move toward the soccer field. A boy in a kilt walks beside a girl with a Hula-Hoop. A woman Ruby recognizes from the Night Owls holds the hand of a man Ruby thinks was one of the fire truck drivers. The redheaded family joins a cluster of boys in ball caps. People mix and shift and sort into new groups, new formations. Finally, Nero appears, walking head down, up the hill toward the old playground. When he gets there, he stands close enough to hear conversation, but no closer. He waits. Lucy waits.

"I made a wish on Captain Bunning's statue,"

says Ruby, finally. "It was supposed to come true at the parade, but it didn't."

"It didn't?" Nero looks surprised. "I thought when you got quiet up there—"

"I still don't know what the wish was," says Lucy. Her voice sounds hard.

Nero matches the sound. "I don't either, okay?"

So Ruby tells about Gigi's last day, about being so sad, about how she made her wish. All the while Nero has been coming closer, until finally he is sitting on the carousel too.

"I stood up there on that float and listened and all I heard was regular stuff. Nothing changed." Ruby feels her eyes pricking up.

"You know," says Lucy, after a minute, "it's still Bunning Day."

"That's right!" Nero leaps to his feet. "The wish comes true before Bunning Day is *over!* There are still more than three hours left! You could try again!"

From the carousel, Ruby can see the schoolhouse float. There are people all around it, including an Event Staff person whose job it is to make sure nobody touches the fake school. "I couldn't get up there again. Nobody'd let me."

Lucy follows Ruby's eyes. "Why do you have to do it up there?"

"That's why I was chosen Essay Girl. Because of the wish. It was a sign."

"Maybe it was a sign that you wrote a good essay," says Nero.

"Tell me again what your wish was," Lucy says.

"I wished that I could go back and fix things—that I could do what I was supposed to have done and listen to Gigi and know what she wanted to say and what she meant and that our last conversation wasn't me not listening."

Nero looks amazed. "You said all that ninety times?"

Ruby shakes her head. "I just wished everything was the way it was supposed to be."

"Supposed to," Lucy says. "So that's—"

"Yeah," says Ruby. "Kind of a wasted wish."

Nero looks puzzled but doesn't ask any questions. He just sits next to Ruby, who sits next to

Lucy. Over at the new playground, moms and dads are gathering their children. "It's getting late," they say. In a nearby tree, a crow caws and then lifts in flight.

Lucy's brow is squinched up — it is the same look that Ruby gets sometimes when she is working on a difficult math problem. "Gigi said, 'Listen'?"

"She said, 'Listen.'" Ruby hears it in her head again. What Gigi said. How it sounded. "And she made a little noise — like a gasp, but she did that a lot on the oxygen — and said, 'It's all coming together.'"

"What does that mean?" asks Nero.

"I don't know. I thought I'd know when my wish came true . . ." It all sounds so stupid. The whole thing. Her wish and what she thought would happen. They must think she's completely nuts. So much for the girl who figures things out.

"You should try it again," Lucy says. "Try listening again."

"I don't —"

"We'll listen too. If you want," says Nero.

Lucy takes Ruby's left hand and closes her eyes tight. Nero closes his eyes too, and a second later Ruby feels his hand on hers. She is suddenly spinny again, except different. Her feet are firmly on the ground. She is rooted to the carousel, held in place by the hands of her friends.

Ruby closes her eyes. She does not think it will make any difference, but if Lucy and Nero are willing to try, she supposes she could too. "Okay," Ruby says. "I'm listening."

In the distance she hears the sounds of little kids at the other playground. Laughter from the soccer field. The clank and clatter of folding chairs. People call to one another across the parking lot, and somewhere a bunch of kids are singing the gingerbread song. Then she hears Lucy, who cannot help but try out Gigi's lines.

"It's *all* coming together. It's all *coming* together. *It's* all coming together," she whispers. Each time it sounds different. Each time it means something different. It's all coming *together*.

If you were Ruby Pepperdine, you might feel a

poke just then. You might hear Lucy whisper, "It's all coming together." Hear how it makes the meaning change to something like it's all *about* coming together, which is something you can imagine Gigi saying. Like maybe that was what Gigi meant, and maybe that is what she would have said more clearly if you'd have just listened.

And maybe that is not what Gigi meant, and maybe you are making it up because you want so much for your wish to come true.

It's all *about* coming together. Ruby and Gigi. Gigi and all her organizations and groups and friends. All the people, all the places, all of Bunning coming together. Gigi *would* say this, Ruby knows with absolute certainty. Even if it was not what Gigi was trying to say that morning, it is something she would say, and mean with all her heart.

If you were Ruby Pepperdine, you might take a deep breath then.

You might listen extra hard.

And then you might open your eyes.

Constellations

⊙ ◉ ⊙

Over the years, Ruby will think about that moment. About Nero and Lucy and about whether or not her wish had come true and she had heard what Gigi wanted to say. She will wonder whether she had done what she was supposed to do. Sometimes she will think that she must have, and other times — like when she has fallen off her bike, or a boy has broken her heart, or she can't find her house key — she will think she must not have. But most of the time, she will think that there really isn't a supposed to at all. That all she can do is her best at any particular moment. And that sometimes that will lead to things feeling great, and sometimes it will not. And that is as supposed to as it gets.

That night, while the Bunning Day sky turned dark as the blueberry filling in a Delish donut, things went this way: Ruby sat in the middle of a blanket, her legs outstretched, leaning back on her hands. To her left was Lucy, just where she had always been. And to her right was Nero, whose parents said he could sit with his friends this year.

"Do you remember which one Leo is?" asks Lucy, staring up at the stars.

Ruby tries, but she cannot. She can find the Big Dipper and the Little Dipper and Cassiopeia, but she cannot find Leo.

"Who named the constellations, anyway?" asks Nero. "I mean, really. The Ancient Greeks, sure. But which ones? What were they thinking about?"

Ruby knows this. Gigi had told her. "They were characters from myths. From stories. The Greeks saw their stories in the sky. Probably the Mayans did too. And the Vikings."

"Well, I'm going to make my own constellation," says Nero. And he tries. But it is difficult to point out an entire constellation to someone else. Gigi could do it, of course, but Ruby is not about to suggest that Nero wrap his arm around her and point.

Finally, he finds a bright star — one that is a little bit purplish — and Lucy and Ruby and Nero all agree that they are looking at the same one.

"I'm starting there," he says. "I'm naming that star."

"Let me guess," says Lucy. "You're naming it Nero."

"It's a little flashy for me, actually. Looks more like a Lucy."

"Oh," says Lucy. She says it only once, but it seems to carry a bunch of meanings. "Okay. And that one to the right of it? That's Ruby."

"And the one a little farther over that way," says Ruby, pointing, "that's Nero."

It is not so complicated keeping those three

stars in their sights. Lucy, Ruby, and Nero. It is not so hard to imagine the invisible connections between them — though Ruby does not draw them straight, like the lines between the stars in Orion or Leo or Cassiopeia. Ruby's lines curve.

"Together," she says, "they are the constellation 'the Donut.'"

Nero laughs. "Take that, Callimachus," he says, but nobody hears him. Instead, they hear a *BOOM*, which rattles in each of their chests and resets their heartbeats. *BOOM!* And a *screeeeeech* — and a bright light streaks high above them and crackles like a million billion stars — like a million billion stars exploding into being.

If you had been sitting on the blanket then, you might have seen their faces in the light of those stars, seen their eyes reflecting it all. Seen their mouths open in momentary awe. You might have felt like you understood something at that moment. At the beginning of The Hole Shebang.

Ruby Pepperdine, however, sees none of these

things. Her eyes are looking up. Her ears are filled with the crackle of new stars.

If you stopped watching her, you might see it yourself. You might hear it, too. Hear it all coming together.

Listen.

A Note from the Author

◉ ◉ ◉

I made up the story of Captain Bunning's invention of the donut hole after hearing about Captain Hanson Gregory, a Maine sailor who, legend says, in 1847 rescued his own donuts in a manner similar to the one described in this book. Other stories claim that Captain Gregory simply got fed up with the undercooked middles of his donuts and proposed eliminating the situation altogether by cutting holes in the dough cakes before frying. There is evidence of holed donuts in times prior to this as well. Should you be spurred to a life of donut-centric archaeology as a result of the desire to learn the true origins of the donut hole, I wish you a fruitful and delicious career.

Since you know now that I made up the whole Captain Bunning donut thing, you've probably figured out that there is no Bunning, New Hampshire, either, and thus no statue and no bronze donut through which one might toss a wishful quarter. But here's the thing about wishes — they don't really require legends and rules and figuring out. All they need is someone to wish them.

Sometimes we don't even know how to wish for the things we need most. When I was a sixth-grader, I could not have known to wish for all the wonderful people at Houghton Mifflin Harcourt who have made my writing career so fun. Thankfully, the wish wasn't required and I lucked out — especially with my editor, Jeannette Larson.

I also would not have thought to wish for all the talented writer and reader friends who critiqued this story and helped make it better: Myra Wolfe, Susan Stewart, Kelly Fineman, Leda Schubert, Ellen Miles, Loree Griffin Burns, and Kate and Ella Messner. I lucked out there, too.

I know that when I was young, I wished I'd grow up and marry a sweet guy and have a couple of nice kids. My reality turned out so much better than my wish. Julio, Jack, and Claire, you are not only sweet and nice, but funny, curious, inspiring, supportive, and rather good-looking. I am so grateful to be in your constellation.

LINDA URBAN's

debut novel, *A Crooked Kind of Perfect*,
was selected for many best-books lists and was
nominated for twenty state awards. Her novel
Hound Dog True received four starred reviews
and was named a Kirkus Best Book of 2011.
A former bookseller, she lives in
Montpelier, Vermont, with her family.
www.lindaurbanbooks.com